SARAH MARSH

EVERNIGHT PUBLISHING ®

www.evernightpublishing.com

Copyright© 2018

Sarah Marsh

Editor: Karyn White

Cover Artist: Jay Aheer

ISBN: 978-1-77339-578-4

SARAH MARSH

DEDICATION

First, a huge thank you to some awesome ladies who have read this book almost as many times as I have while it was being written. Amy, Elena, and Maia, I love you guys!

Second, thank you to my mother, who has put up with my sass and sarcasm all my life. Dori is basically a manifestation of the little voice inside my head that sometimes gets me into trouble, so perhaps by giving her an alternate outlet my mouth will start to behave. Either way, I'm pretty sure you've earned some kind of award for your patience mom…I'll look into that. ☺

SARAH MARSH

VIKTOR

Happy Evil After, 1

Sarah Marsh

Copyright © 2017

Prologue

My name is Pandora. I'm a dark Fairy Godmother.

What—never heard of a dark Fairy Godmother, you say? Well, that's because only about one in every one million Fairy Godmother pregnancies result in a blending of wild magic that ends up with a deviant like me.

I still remember that day at health class in Godmother finishing school…

"Girls! Make sure you never trust a boy when he says, 'Don't you trust me, baby?' And once you're bonded, never have sex in any other position other than missionary!"

Yeesh, have you *seen* how the Fairy Godfathers dress around here? Prancing around in their pastel leggings and embroidered velvet frocks? No freaking thank you. I'd rather have sex with the Gnome gardener that was always peeping in the girls' locker room than let one of those dandies get at me.

Apparently, it runs in the family because my mother was a badass, too. All she's ever told me about my father was that on one spring break, she and her fellow sorority sisters, The Raging Blue Fairies, decided to do something crazy. They flew down to Florida, hit the paranormal bars that were "happening" at the time, had a few too many Mai Tais, ended up in the hot tub with a dashing male of the *non-fairy* variety. One thing led to another, and nine months later I came into the world. In a true fashion that only I can pull off, she said, I unfurled my smoke-grey and black wings and gave the head nurse the finger before starting to cry.

The ruling Fairy Godmother Council, of course, tried to make my mom give me up, since not only was she *not* bonded, but I was the epitome of all that could go wrong in the life of a Fairy Godmother. There was no such thing as a Fairy with black wings. "Darkling magic" they whispered. They wanted her to leave me in the woods for the Sprites to decide my fate and let the realm reabsorb my magic if that was its will. But like I said, my mom was badass, and she very politely, because she was still a Fairy Godmother, told them to shove off and curled her sparkly blue wings around me.

While my mom always made sure that I knew she loved me just the way I am, I never really did fit in with our society. It's totally true what they say about me, I *do* create havoc and trouble where ever I go. And … I freaking love doing it! I spent most of my school days punking the other Fairy God-students, and even the teachers weren't safe from my wrath.

Before you bring it up—I was *not* the one who opened that damned box of sins. The fucking thing was already open when I strolled into the girls' locker room. I think those damned Pink Pixies set me up. It had only been a week since I drugged them in the chemistry lab and shaved off all their eyebrows. Who knew they would be so vindictive?

I almost felt like we could've been friends after

that. Too bad.

Eventually, I did get kicked out of school, but not before I absorbed one very clear fact that I took great offense to within my mother's society of do-gooders. They used their magic to help others find their happy endings, but not *all* others, just the "good" people who they decided deserved it.

Who were these pompous assholes that got to decide that, just because someone takes a less-than-understood path in their life, they were "evil" and not deserving of a happy ending? Well, I call bullshit on that, bitches.

See, I have my own brand of power, and I decided that *I* would be the Fairy Godmother picking up the slack for all the misunderstood "monsters and villains" out there. After all, they're simply different just like me, right? And let me tell you, I make damn sure I get *my* happy ending on the regular if you know what I mean. *wink*

****

"Hey, Dori, what are ya writing?" Craig, the demon bartender, nodded towards my black matchmaking mastermind notebook as he slid my frosty Chi Chi over the bar. "Are you finally going to write a 'How to' book on having your pick of the para-men litter?"

"Har, har, Craig. You know, it's a good thing you know how to use that tongue of yours for something other than sassing me or I might just have to wish it away." I smirked at my sometimes-casual hookup, at least for the nights when I didn't find anything better in this place.

The Pit is the most notorious paranormal bar around, famous for its deviants and surprisingly enough, Craig's super delicious fruity drinks. I've been coming here since I was a teenager. It is an exceptionally good hunting ground when a gal wanted a little company of the temporary bad-boy variety. I know all the regulars, and I knew exactly who I would choose to be my first lucky project.

"So, Craig, tell me everything you know about Mr. Tall, Dark, and Bitey over there," I said nodding towards the broody vamp in the corner of the bar.

Craig's eyes went wide when he saw who I was asking about, and then he just shook his head at me.

"I think he might be a little too wild even for you, Dori. You don't want to tangle with the likes of him," he answered quietly, almost as if my quarry might hear him through this entire racket, even on the other side of the room.

Truthfully, I wondered myself for a second if he might be able to. Viktor Krescech was the monster under the bed for our kind. Paranormal parents scared their kids with stories of him at night when they were being bad and wouldn't go to sleep. He was The Destroyer of Covens, a ruthless killer of anyone who got in his way. He was also notorious for his hatred of his own kind. Now that was just plain un-neighborly.

Being the selfless and dedicated overachiever that I was, I had already given my new career path a great deal of serious thought and of course realized that my so-called "clients" would most likely rebuff any offers of matchmaking bliss … no doubt violently. So all I had to do was find out what would motivate them to be exactly where they needed to be, the exact moment that my kick-ass fairy powers proclaimed as the lynchpin for their happy ending. It seemed easy really.

After all, I've always had superior "people management" skills … even if my mom just called it "being a shifty, little manipulator".

VIKTOR

Skills are skills; that's what I say. How hard could this be?

Chapter One

"Hey there, Halle-cat, where are you sneaking off to?"

"Fuck, Tavin!" Halle must have jumped about four feet straight in the air, much to her brothers' amusement, "Balls, why do you insist on sneaking up on me like that?"

"Because, you jump like a cartoon cat." He smirked as he leaned against the wall in the hallway with his arms crossed. "It's too funny not to do it, really."

"You're such a dick—even for an older brother."

"You're avoiding the question. Where are you going? You know Dad wants everyone here for this dinner. He said it's important."

Halle sighed. Like her brother could really understand what it felt like to be her at these Pard events. To the males she wasn't related to, she was untouchable—and therefore invisible. Why bother talking to the girl whose father would castrate you if you touched her? On the other hand, those men who weren't part of her father's pard only looked at her in two ways: like she was a curious science experiment or a female out to trap them.

After all, what shifter male wanted to take the chance on fooling around with a female who wasn't his mate if there was a possibility of knocking her up? No one, that's who. She was cursed by the Briggs family legacy.

"The vamps give me the heebie-jeebies, you know that." She gave her big brother her biggest Puss in Boots eyes she could manage without popping something. "Can't you cover for me, just this once?"

"Sorry, kiddo." Tavin reached out and messed up her hair because he knew it drove her nuts. "The old man says it's all hands on deck. Come on, we can get drunk on champagne and make fun of everyone."

"Fine." She smacked his hands away and tried to smooth out her unruly curls. "But we're playing the 'dub-over' game, and if any of those blood suckers hear us you have to take the rap with dad."

They'd been playing the "dub-over" game since they were kids every time their parents forced them to attend these boring dinners and parties. It was hilarious to choose their hoity-toity victims and then turn their no-doubt inane conversation into something that would have them laughing until they cried—but with shifter hearing being as good as it was, they'd spent a lot of hours grounded in their rooms because of it.

As they grew up and threw alcohol into the mix, not to mention a filthier vocabulary, the game changed into trying to get your competitor to lose his or her composure in front of a room full of guests. Halle was going to play extra hard this evening if Tavin was going to make her attend. Maybe there was a vamp in the crowd tonight that was looking for a little companionship of the male leopard variety?

Tavin didn't swing that way, but damn, wouldn't it be funny seeing him try to diplomatically rebuff a few unwanted advances. *I am so doing this.*

"Deal." Her brother's eyes narrowed in suspicion when she couldn't contain her deviant grin, but it was too late for him now. Plan "Make the big bad vamps think Tavin likes a little sausage on sausage slap and tickle" had officially commenced.

"Now go get changed into something frilly." Tavin's eyes went huge as he ducked the boot that came flying at his head right before Halle slammed her bedroom door in his face.

Twenty minutes later, they were guzzling daddy's

finest champagne while trying to avoid actually interacting with any of the "guests".

"Nice dress, kiddo, are you hitting a funeral later?"

"Oh, should I have dressed like *that*, do you think?" She looked pointedly in the direction of the group of vampires who'd just arrived, the females barely covering their assets in tiny dresses that looked to be made out of dinner napkins.

"Hell no, I'd have to gouge my eyes out if I ever saw you dressed like that." Her brother cringed before taking a longer look at the lady-vamps. "But I'm not saying I'd kick *them* out of my bed for eating crackers—*if* you know what I mean?"

"First of all, idiot," she laughed, "by the looks of those front two, they wouldn't be eating anything in your bed that left crumbs. Second, just make sure you pay their pimp first. Daddy would be awfully upset if his male heir *did* happen to get eaten by hookers."

"True enough, looks like the Coven Master has all the moves."

They stood and watched from their perch on the second-floor balcony overlooking the foyer, as their parents greeted the smarmy looking vampire at the front of the group, the sickly thin females draped on each of his arms. Halle wasn't overly fond of vampires to begin with—well, she didn't know many in truth, but they just seemed so dramatically different than shifters like her.

Halle almost squeaked when her father motioned the vamp's attention up towards her and Tavin. The noise turned to a snarl as the bastard handed his arm candy off to his henchmen like they were a coat and hat, not living beings, before the two men wandered off in the direction of the bar area, much to Halle's relief. She'd been terrified that her father would bring him over to introduce them and she'd be forced to act polite, as if she hadn't just watched the douchebag drop off his hoes-to-go for the evening. *Ew.* Her "polite face" only went so far.

"So how do you know that was the Coven Master?" she whispered to her brother.

"His name is Conrad Dair. Father has met with him before, and I went along with him last time," he answered, his face oddly serious for her jester of a sibling. "I can't say that I liked him very much."

Halle took a long look at the man who walked beside her father. He was almost as tall as her dad, but nowhere near as wide, his frame was more wiry than buff. His short blond hair was slicked back with way too much product, and his face was clean-shaven. All in all, there was nothing about him that screamed "unattractive"—it was just something in his dark eyes that made her not trust him. He looked like one of those guys that after they snapped their bolt and mass murdered the entire neighborhood, one of their third-grade teachers would be interviewed saying, "Oh but he was such a quiet boy…"

Right before they entered the next room, Conrad Dair looked up and zeroed in right on her. His dark eyes staring intently at her in the most uncomfortable way, it felt like an eternity before he broke his gaze and followed along behind her father.

"Well, that was *horrifying.*" Tavin frowned. "I think it's time to hit the tequila and then see if we can't escape quietly."

"Yes, please." She grabbed onto her brother's arm, desperately needing the reassurance of his touch. Never again did she want to be the undivided focus of that man's attention if she could help it.

Chapter Two

It's happening.

Dori sat straight up from the couch she'd been dozing on. Finally, it was time. Her magic was telling her that the clock had just begun on her first project, and now there was only so much time she had to manipulate her clients into making all the right decisions—or the Happy Ever After they sought would slip out of their reach forever.

"Ma! I gotta go out," she yelled towards the kitchen as she gathered her phone and shoved it into her purse.

"Where are you going? I thought we were going to make some popcorn and watch *Game of Thrones*?" Her mom frowned as she popped her head around the corner to look at her. "If you take off, I'm still watching it. I won't be the only one at work tomorrow not knowing what happened!"

"Fine," Dori sighed, throwing her hands up, "I'll watch it when I get back—alone, like a leper. But you'd better make damned sure that you don't accidentally hit delete after you watch it, Mom!"

"I *told* you, I didn't do that on purpose! It's just natural instinct to delete the shows on the PVR once you've watched them."

"I can never get back those episodes of *Penny Dreadful*! I only watched them once, and now that the last season is done there's no telling how long it'll be before they replay the entire series." She pouted, and this time it was her mom's turn to roll her eyes.

"Why don't you just stream them online?"

Dori gasped, her hand coming up to her throat in shock. "What am I, some kind of hipster who's trying to stick it to the 'man' by refusing to pay for cable? Ew,

Mom, shame on you. I'm not watching Eva Green on a seventeen-inch computer screen like an animal. She's better than that—we *both* are."

"Fine! I'll wait exactly two hours … but if you're not back by ten I'm watching it!"

"Cool." Dori smiled and headed for the front door, "See ya at 9:55—and don't forget to make fresh popcorn!"

****

Halle looked back over her shoulder towards the ground that was two floors below her. Perhaps she had miscalculated on her inherent feline abilities to "always land on her feet". If she dropped from this height, she had a feeling that her curvy body might end up in a chalk outline on the pavement instead of making the sneaky getaway she'd intended. She was hanging from her second story bedroom window and, to be quite honest, was more than a little bit stuck.

Well, fuck me, she thought.

Just as she was contemplating whether or not to alert her father's guards and call for help, the window at her knees opened up and strong arms pulled her back inside the house that used to be her safe haven.

"What in the hell are you doing out there, Halle?" Tavin said, as he put her down on the couch in the living room just in time for her father to storm into the room.

"For Goddess's sake, Halle, are you trying to get yourself killed?" her dad yelled as he shut the window behind them.

"I might as well die. You're condemning me to a life of enslavement. A life without a true mating by agreeing to give me to that criminal!" she yelled back, furious at the announcement her father had made at dinner tonight.

Halle almost felt bad at her accusation when she

saw the look of torment on her father's face before he looked away. She knew it couldn't have been easy for him to agree to the terms of the Coven Master's request. The entire Briggs family knew that fateful day when the leader of the North American coven had just "happened" to be in the right place at the right time to rescue Halle's father from a group of rogue vampires, that one day he'd come forward to claim the blood debt and they'd be powerless not to agree to whatever he asked of them.

In the paranormal community, Halle's family was known for two things: her father was the alpha of the largest leopard pard on the west coast, and that the Briggs line was one of a few magical families that seemed to be able to procreate across species borders outside of a true mating.

This meant that Halle, being the only daughter of a very powerful man, with the eggs to match no less, was a pretty hot commodity. Unfortunately for her, it wasn't because of who she was as a person. It was all about the uterus. Growing up she'd never even been allowed to date anyone who wasn't preapproved by her parents, which left a pretty big gap in her social life experience. Between her father and her brother scaring the ever-living shit out of any boy who looked at her with interest, she was now about to be carted off to a strange vampire as a virgin bride.

She'd only seen the Coven Master Conrad Dair that once, at her parents' party, and had been instantly creeped out by how intently he'd stared at her, like if he looked hard enough he could actually impregnate her right there in front of everyone. She knew that she would be a means to an end for him. He hadn't even had a conversation with her and yet he wanted to marry her?

Yeah, right. Halle might have been inexperienced, but she wasn't stupid. That leech wanted to turn her into his own little hybrid breeding machine, and she wasn't going to have any of it.

"You know we would never accept this if we had any choice, Halle." Her father's tormented voice brought tears to her eyes. "But we cannot win in a war with the vampires, and his blood debt must be answered. I'm so sorry, darling. If I could go back, I would have accepted my fate and not taken his help when offered."

That statement from her father had both of them tearing up. She didn't want to marry a stranger, but she couldn't wish her father had died that night. Halle knew she had to walk into the custody of Conrad's guards tomorrow of her own free will, for her family and for the rest of their pard. She'd just have to come up with another way to foil her fiancé's plans that would keep her family off the hook. How hard could *that* be?

Chapter Three

Viktor could tell from the twitchiness of the bartender when his pint was dropped off that someone in this bar had been asking after him. *Good.* A fight was just what he needed tonight. Well, not that it was ever much of a fight, but he could really use a little venting that was for sure. He'd been so dreadfully bored the last few years.

He spent a few moments eyeing the rest of the patrons to try to guess who he may get to beat the hell out of later. Was it the smarmy looking incubus over by the ladies' washroom? He deserved it just for trying to pick up women coming out of the bathroom. The creep factor alone on that move was disgusting.

Oh, look! There was a table of three bruiser wolf shifters. Now *that* looked like a fun fight. Shifters were such a plucky bunch, and they certainly could take a hit. Viktor silently hoped it was them.

He certainly wasn't expecting the sexy goth chick that normally sat at the bar to saunter on up to his table and help herself to a chair.

"So, handsome, are you out celebrating your Coven Master's crowning achievement tonight?" she asked, as she took a sip of her fruity drink, which appeared to have an airplane of pineapple sitting along the rim.

What kind of a bartender makes an airplane out of pineapple?

Viktor was just trying to figure out if *he* could make an airplane out of fruit when her comment suddenly registered in his brain.

What the hell did she just ask me? He had to hold himself back from snarling at her, as if *he* would ever kneel to any coven leader. Clearly, this girl was crazy because no one who knew of his reputation with Conrad would ever dare to assume that bastard held any authority over Viktor—and anyone who came to this bar as much as she did would know who he was. Back in the day, he'd taken the heads of hundreds of Paras for even mentioning Conrad's name in front of him. It was just very lucky for her that he had a little-known policy of not hurting innocent women or children.

"I assure you, I have no coven leader, and I have *no* idea what you are talking about," he growled out. "Now leave me be."

"Really? Oh wow, that's embarrassing. My bad," she said in a tone that suggested that she was indeed not sorry at all. "Word on the Fairy Godmother pipeline is that Conrad is getting the means to his 'Happy Ever After' tomorrow. I just assumed that all the local vamps would be stoked for him."

What was this? That lying, sociopathic bastard Conrad was getting a Happy-fucking-Ever After? The same Coven Master of North America who had killed more innocents than the black plague? One who *still* didn't hesitate to kill anyone who stood in the way of what he wanted? How was this possible?

No. There was no way that Viktor would sit back and let this happen. Conrad was the last living member of the coven that had turned him and ruined his life. A monster like that did not deserve happiness... Viktor should know because *he* was a monster as well.

He hadn't always been one, though. Once upon a time, he had been just a normal man like any other. In his mortal life, he'd begun as a farmer, much like his father, but then the Empire came calling and one simply did not say "no" to Rome. Viktor did what he must to keep his family safe, and he soon realized that he was a much better warrior than he'd ever been a farmer. Still, the goal had been as always, to survive his conscripted years and get back to his wife and young son.

They'd been marching for days, somewhere in northern Europe. Their Captain had ordered them to make camp for the night, and they were all relieved for the break and despite the cold, Viktor had fallen asleep almost immediately. He had woken hours later by the screams of his fellow soldiers all around him. It had sounded like a pack of rabid animals was attacking. The snarls and roars were louder than anything he'd ever heard before, and he'd immediately grabbed his sword and dashed out of the tent, only to find that it wasn't animals at all that were attacking them, but beings unlike anything he'd ever seen.

They moved so fast he could barely track them with his eyes, and their teeth and claws were long and sharp. He saw one of his troop ripped almost completely in half by one of these feral creatures, and he did not hesitate to cleave its unholy head from its body. He fought for hours it seemed, until finally, he came across a woman standing amongst the carnage, watching all that death happen with a doting smile as if her children were playing at the oceanside. She was the most beautiful woman he'd ever seen, and when she met his eyes he lost the will to raise his sword against her.

That was the first time the she-demon had taken his will from him, but it was far from the last, and he'd wished a thousand times over that he'd never laid eyes on that creature. Melisandre had been enamored of his ferocity and had decided to take him as a pet, even as she condemned every single other soldier to death that night. Viktor had been her blood servant and her sex slave for five tormented years before she finally decided that he was getting old and that she would turn him to keep him with her forever. She wasn't prepared, however, for the depth of his hatred and rage. As soon as she had turned him, he'd risen from his new birth in a frenzy of carnage and slaughtered the entire coven in retribution. All save for one cowardly, conniving male who'd gotten away. Conrad.

Viktor had spent his first couple of centuries tracking down other covens in search of the sneaky bastard, slaughtering them all. He had been utterly mad in those first years, so lost in the grief of having his family and his mortality stolen from him. He could never go home again being the monster they had created. With his lust for blood, he would never trust himself around his wife and child. For years he'd hunted tirelessly, for all vampires were the enemy in this new existence he endured. It wasn't until a couple of decades later and thousands of deaths that he'd recovered enough mentally and emotionally to realize that not all paranormals were evil. Just like humans, there was good with the bad. By that time his actions had reached all across the Para community, so most avoided him if possible, and others actively hunted him, which only increased his skills and cunning.

Eventually, he found himself back to almost his mortal temperament, although he still chose to keep to himself mostly. Trust wasn't something that came easily for him, and he figured he was better safe than sorry. He'd learned over his immortal life that others would try to kill him just to say that they had. Reputations were a double-edged sword that way. The whispered tales of the monster he'd been kept some at bay, but there were always a few who came looking for trouble and he would oblige them. He didn't even feed off of anyone who wasn't a killer anymore, but he didn't dare tell anyone that. After all, reputation was everything, right?

Viktor had moved to the United States from

Europe about eighty years ago when Conrad had finally turned up and been ridiculously appointed as Coven Leader of North America. The previous leader had met a suspiciously untimely death, and apparently, Conrad had been pretending to *not* be a complete sociopath and playing the role of first lieutenant long enough that there was no longer anyone on the Para Council who remembered what a monster he really was.

They had no idea about all the crimes against para and human beings alike that he had committed or who they were putting into power. Viktor had spent years trying to find a way to finally kill the bastard. Unfortunately, he'd never found a way to get to Conrad after the asshole had moved into the newly appointed home that came with the job. It would have been a suicide trip into his compound with the sheer numbers of vampires he had turned. But if there was something he could do to make sure that the bastard didn't get what he wanted, well then, Viktor would do it.

"Stop," he said as the crazy girl was about to turn and leave. "Tell me everything that you know about Conrad's 'Happy Ever After'."

As she sat back down, he could've sworn he saw a devious smile cross her lips, but then again, she was obviously a few bricks short of a load to have sat down at his table in the first place.

Chapter Four

Halle was exhausted, more so emotionally than physically, although hanging out from her bedroom window was a bit more exercise than she typically enjoyed. She could only shake her head as she thought about the family blowout that had just happened downstairs. Her mother had barged in shortly after her rescue and then proceeded to cry for forty minutes because her "baby was going to get married to some horrible stranger". So as per usual, things went from being about her to being about how traumatized her mother was. Cripes, how could she have come from the loins of such a drama-queen?

To add insult to injury, when she opened her bedroom door and turned on the lights, there was a strange goth girl with black and grey wings sitting on her bed staring at her. Halle was so startled she almost screamed.

"Hello, Halle!" the stranger said, as she motioned her hand towards the door and it swung shut behind her.

"Who the hell are you, and why are you in my room?" Halle asked as her hackles rose and her claws slid out of her fingertips.

"Goddess, kitty, no need to get all aggro," she answered as she bounced a few times on the bed. "I'm your Fairy Godmother of course!"

The girl is clearly insane was all that went through Halle's mind as the female's black eyes stared up at her expectantly. Batshit crazy or not, this being obviously had some strong magic, and Halle knew better than to bring her claws to a fireball fight. So, how do you get a crazy magical woman out of your house without getting turned into a toad or something?

So she did what all cats do when uncertain about

what to do—she froze.

"Halle," the woman said with a dramatic sigh, "seriously. We need to figure out a way to get you out of this whole mess. You cannot marry Conrad. He's a bit of a dick, you know?"

Those were the magic words for Halle. She didn't care who this person was now, not if she was going to help her get the hell away from that leech.

"Right?" Halle said in exasperation as she jumped onto the bed next to her new friend. "I *knew* he was a dick! But how am I going to get out of this without starting a war, Fairy God … umm, person?"

"You can call me Dori," she answered with a wink. "I have the perfect plan that will screw Conrad over, get you your Happy Ending, *and* launch my new career all in one strategic move!"

Wait a minute, Halle thought. *New career?*

"Hey… do you know what you're doing? This is not just my life we're talking about but my family's, too. Can you pull this off?" she asked narrowing her eyes at the fairy.

"Of course, I can! I've already got your rescuer primed and ready to go," Dori said with a roll of her eyes. "But we're going to need snacks while we plan this out."

One wave of the odd Fairy Godmother's hand and there was a spread of junk food settled between them on the bed. All of Halle's favorites were there.

"You know, I always thought that Fairy Godmothers were stuffy little old lady fairies, but you're kind of awesome," Halle said as she settled in so they could plan her escape.

"*I know*, right?" Dori said as she popped open a bag of chips. "So here's the plan, and you're going to have to stick to your guns on this one because your fated mate is a stubborn S.O.B. and he will probably try to send you on your way for 'your own good'. But no matter what, do *not* let him shake you loose or this entire thing is going to go to shit. I've looked at all the angles, and this is your one shot at a happy ending, do you understand me, Halle?"

Both Halle's human side and her cat fully understood that this was their shot at a real mating, and they both would do whatever was necessary. She'd get her happy ending and her family and pard would be safe from Conrad's machinations.

"So, who is my mate then?" Halle asked excitedly as she helped herself to a big mouthful of peanut butter M&M's.

"Viktor Krescech, and bitch, you must have a horseshoe up that lucky ass of yours because he is *smoking* hot!" Dori answered waggling her eyebrows right before a mouthful of wet M&M's came spitting at her face. "*Dude!* That's just offside!"

Halle hacked and coughed as she tried to expel the handful of candies that had just been sucked into her windpipe when Dori said that name.

"Are you fucking crazy? Viktor *The Destroyer* is my mate?" she wheezed out, tears running down her face. "He's a psychopath with a reputation worse than Conrad!"

"Now just calm down, no need to be a spazzy-cat," Dori said, handing her a bottle of water to clear the candy pieces still rattling around in her throat. "Don't you trust me? His reputation, while totally justified when he was first turned, is mostly just rumor and propaganda now. He's not actually a bad guy. He won't even feed off anyone who isn't a douchebag anymore. He's just misunderstood really."

Halle was still a bit suspicious, but Dori *was* her

Fairy Godmother after all. I mean, if a girl couldn't trust her own Fairy Godmother, then what was this world coming to?

"All right, I'm taking your word on it for now, but he better be really hot," she finally answered. "Now how do we do this? Conrad's goons are picking me up tomorrow."

Chapter Five

Viktor calmly waited on top of the office building, at the corner of Mission Street and Hyack Boulevard, just as the crazy woman had told him to. It was ten minutes until noon. She had said that Conrad's men would stop in the ally precisely at noon, and he was to collect whatever was inside this car if he wanted to foil his nemesis's only chance at a Happy Ever After.

He wasn't quite sure he believed the odd little fairy, but he wasn't going to risk missing the opportunity either. It certainly wouldn't cost him anything to sit up here and check it out. The propaganda that vampires would spontaneously combust in the sun was of course just that, propaganda. When the Spanish Inquisition was happening in the 1400s, the Para Council had gotten together and "leaked" all sorts of fabricated species tidbits and weaknesses. The information was intended to help the paranormal beings camouflage better amongst the rest of the mortals when the religious fanatics were torturing and killing people at an alarming rate. It couldn't have worked better, and most of those same mythologies were alive and well to this very day.

Vampires burned in the daylight? Nah, but Viktor had to admit that his tan was a bit on the sad side. Could vampires only ingest blood? Of course not, but some of the older ones did get tired of eating food when a liquid diet could be so much more convenient on the go. Each species had their own lore, and it had kept most of them from being hunted by the humans, just as it was designed to.

When he spied the black car pulling into the alleyway he was actually a little surprised. Perhaps that crazy drunk chick was telling him the truth after all. In all the years that Viktor had lived as a vampire, he'd never met a Fairy Godmother.

So naturally, he assumed that they were just a myth created by the fairies to protect their own species. Some sort of "don't kill the fairy because you might not get your happy ending" kind of bullshit. He'd met several run of the mill fairies of course, but nothing quite like her. She'd practically vibrated with magic.

When the front car door opened below him and one of Conrad's lackeys jumped out, quickly pulling open the back door, he realized that finally, his chance was here to ruin Conrad's life. He stepped off the ledge and silently dropped to the ground just in time to see a little blonde head come streaking out of the back seat and bend over in front of the dumpster.

"Gosh, guys, I'm sorry. I really thought I was going to puke. Guess I'm just nervous about the ceremony, huh?" A sweet lilting voice washed over him.

Viktor had to shake his head to get his attention away from the rather shapely ass that was bent over in front of him. He needed his focus back to the four thugs that poured out of the car once he stepped out of the shadows and away from the wall.

"Krescech! What do you want?" the largest vamp said as he saw Viktor approach, immediately putting himself between Viktor and the girl, but not before he caught a glimpse of huge green eyes framed with dark lashes.

"I simply want Conrad to get what he deserves … which would be nothing but a painful death," Viktor answered, taking a step closer, scenting that two of the other guards were also vamps and the third was a wolf. He was already calculating the battle in his head. The only unknown factor would be how the girl would react as he could scent that she was some kind of shifter as well. He was relieved to see her head pop back around the first guard and a smile bloom on her face at his words.

"Get back in the car, girl," the vamp snarled over his shoulder in her direction as he advanced towards Viktor.

He was a big bastard, and it was clear in the way that he moved that he was a fairly new turn. Viktor had never run into him before, but it was amusing that all of Conrad's lackeys knew him on sight. They must have a *Most Wanted* poster of him up in the clubhouse. *How cute.*

That was the problem with the Coven Master being a complete asshole. All of the older vamps didn't put up with his bullshit. So they either left the city or became unaligned rogues like Viktor, leaving Conrad no choice but to create a brand new army of baby vamps. This became an issue when they ended up fighting against immortals that had hundreds of years of battle experience in their favor. The newbies still fought like humans, which meant they died just like them as well … quickly.

It was with a satisfying thud that the first vampire's head dropped to the pavement behind Viktor. The hulk had been going in for a punch to his face, and it was a simple thing to grab Victor's favorite blade from his waist sheath, back turn and slice the metal clean through his adversary's neck. Surprisingly, the wolf was the smartest of the remaining three guards. He turned and hauled ass out of the alley into the busy streets beyond as the other two came at him together. While they may have gotten in a few lucky shots, it wasn't enough to stop him from ending them both within minutes, leaving only piles of ash behind.

"Wow," he heard in a sweet voice from behind him. "You certainly don't mess around, do you?"

The woman didn't sound scared, which was a surprise, but then again shifters were raised in a fairly violent environment so a little death and dismemberment shouldn't be a reason for her to freak out.

"I mean you no harm, lady. You can go. I'm only here for what's in the car," he said slowly walking towards her. She was a cute little thing, all soft curves with golden skin and hair.

"Um, yeah, about that … *I'm* what's in the car, Mr. Krescech. You have to take me with you out of here," she said almost nervously, those big green eyes pleading with him.

Clearly, she was *also* insane. What was with the women he was running into this week? Viktor had had more than his fair share of groupies throwing themselves at him in the bars, wanting to take a walk on the wild side for a few hours, but this wholesome little beauty certainly didn't look like the type, so he had no idea exactly what she was asking him for.

"I don't think so," he said, moving past her towards the open back door to search the car.

"Seriously, there's nothing else in the car. They were taking me from my family and my pard to be married to Conrad. I have to go with you to get away from him," she continued, putting her tiny little hands on her very curvy hips in a way that distracted him far more than it should have.

Interesting, so this little number was a leopard shifter? Viktor hadn't really had any interaction with the pard in this country, but by reputation, they were a good lot. Why on Earth would she agree to marry Conrad?

"I don't rescue damsels in distress. I eat them," he said with a flash of fang. "So run along, little kitten."

The tiny spitfire threw her hands dramatically up in the air and sighed loudly.

"You just saved me from a life of baby-making slavery. Aren't you supposed to whisk me away to your super-secret villain lair and ravish me? Sheesh, where's your follow-through?"

Viktor just stood there and stared at her for a moment. He didn't know whether to laugh at her ridiculous statement or take her up on her offer and bend her over right here on the trunk of Conrad's car. He was extremely turned on by the fact that she didn't seem the least bit afraid of him. He'd always tried to pretend that his reputation in the paranormal community pleased him, that it helped him by keeping the rabble away. But deep down it bothered him that everyone always thought the worst of him. His honor was just yet another thing that Melisandre and Conrad had stolen from him when they took his mortality.

"Don't you know who I am, woman?" he finally said as she just stood there looking at him expectantly.

"Yes, I know who you are. Who else is capable of keeping me out of Conrad's douchey hands?" she said sounding a little impatient.

"Don't you have a family you can go to?" he asked, still wondering why he was even standing here talking to her.

Well, that wasn't entirely true. Once she'd said the word "slavery" he knew he couldn't leave her to Conrad's tender mercies. Viktor knew more about slavery than he ever wanted to, and no being should ever be held against their will. That and he had seen firsthand what Conrad enjoyed doing to women. It still sickened him to think back to the horrors he'd had to witness as Melisandre's pet.

"If I go back to my family they'd just have to hand me right back over to him again. My pard owes him a blood debt, and I am the payment. I need this to look like Conrad's men lost me in the confrontation with you. This needs to be his fault, as otherwise, it will start a war between my family and his coven," she said, stepping ever closer.

She stood so close now that Viktor could smell the strawberry and coconut scent of her shampoo. *Good Gods, she smells good enough to eat.*

"Why would you think that I should care whether or not this starts a war for your people? I will not be fighting in it," he answered, trying to sound like he didn't care one way or another.

"Because I think that you hate Conrad just as much, if not more than I do, and there's nothing he wants more than to possess me," she answered quietly, her huge green eyes staring right into his grey ones.

She was right of course. There was no one on this Earth that he hated as much as he hated Conrad. That's what he told himself anyway when he ultimately decided he would take the girl with him—whether it was the whole truth about his motivations or not.

"First, tell me how your pard was thoughtless enough to enter into a blood debt with a killer like Conrad?"

"It's not like we had any choice. My father was jumped one night by a bunch of rogues, and Conrad just *happened* to be there to offer his assistance … for a price."

The venom in her voice clearly stated that she suspected they'd been set up. The rogues were most likely paid to attack by Conrad himself. It was a trick the coward had used over and over again.

"Fine," he said with a sigh. "You can come with me, but just until we find somewhere to stash you that Conrad cannot reach you."

"Thank you!" she said with a squeal just before

she reached up and hugged him before he could stop her. "I'm Halle, by the way."

Clearly, his reputation was *never* going to recover from this if anyone saw him being hugged in the alley, but with her luscious frame leaning against his, smelling so sweet, he had a difficult time finding a reason to care.

Chapter Six

Halle had been relieved when Viktor led her back to his car. The sleek, charcoal grey Aston Martin was beautiful and graceful just like the man himself. When Pandora had first told her that her true mate was a vampire she had been terrified that he would want to fly her all over the place and she had never been a fan of heights.

"So how come you don't fly where you need to go instead of driving?" she asked, trying to make conversation since he hadn't said anything since they'd gotten in the car.

"Flying takes energy, just like anything else. I prefer not to waste mine, plus driving makes it easier to blend in with the humans."

After a twenty-minute drive out of the city, they finally arrived at an old gravel road that looked as though it had been closed due to a river washout. She just about peed in her pants when he simply sped up and drove right through the barrier... When they popped out on the other side unscathed she was shocked to see the large, beautiful home that was surrounded by dense forest.

"You could have warned me about the illusion. Goddess, I almost had kittens," she murmured, his answering grin catching her off guard. Who knew Viktor the Destroyer had a sense of humor?

"Well that would have taken the fun out of it for me then, wouldn't it?" he said as he parked the car and came around to open her door for her. "Plus I paid extra for the barricade illusion so I want to make sure to get my money's worth from those extortionist witches."

****

"Wow, this place is really nice," Halle said as she strolled through the huge entryway of Viktor's home. "I was expecting something a little more … well, serial killy to be honest."

"I'm glad you like it," he answered, trying to keep a straight face. Halle's bizarre habit of blurting out whatever was running through her head at the time was exceptionally charming, and he was having a difficult time not engaging her in conversation just to see what she'd say next.

Viktor was also more pleased than he should have been that she admired his home. He was proud of it. He'd spent centuries collecting various art pieces and antiques from all over the world, and he'd found the perfect estate to showcase it all. He'd even done the decorating all himself, though if anyone else knew that he'd have to kill them. Interior decorating didn't really mesh with his bad boy image.

He'd owned hundreds of properties over his lifetime, but this was his favorite by far. He loved the remote location, which was close enough to the city to make it convenient, but far enough to give him his solitude. He took great care in keeping it a secret as he had no intention of ever giving it up. Most places in the past he'd been relieved when it had been compromised and he'd been forced to move somewhere new, but perhaps the impossible had happened and he'd finally gotten tired of running away from life.

Plus, he had every modern convenience here that was imaginable, and a man had to have his toys. One simply could not compare modern living to what life had been like before Viktor was turned. The dreaded memory of the sanitation alone was enough to make him shudder.

He led Halle to one of the guest rooms that had never been used, as he'd never had a guest before. Subconsciously he put her in the room right across from his own suite.

Subconsciously—right. He didn't want to admit to himself that he may have had another motivation for putting her there.

"This will be your room. You can refresh yourself, and I will go down and see about getting us some dinner," he said, turning quickly before he followed her into the bathroom and did something he shouldn't.

He made his way back downstairs and was utterly disgusted with the fact that his butler Gerald almost surprised him as he rounded the corner, all because he was still thinking about what Halle would look like naked in his very expensive shower.

"Sir, Molly said that we have a guest. Of course, I knew she must have been jesting as you aren't known for your entertaining," the older male said in a dry tone.

Gerald and his wife Molly had been with Viktor for over sixty years now. They were house brownies and quite good at what they did, so good in fact that even Viktor had to overlook the incessant sarcasm thrown his way on a regular basis. Brownies sure could be a pain in the ass, but no one pressed a button-down shirt or ran a household quite like they could.

"Funny, Gerald, but yes, we do indeed have a guest," Viktor said as they continued into the kitchen where Molly was just pulling some cookies out of the oven. "Oh, are those oatmeal?"

"Getcher' fingers out, sir!" Molly answered with a smile as she swatted his hand away from the tray.

"But those are my favorite," he said with a frown. This was *his* house, so why was she denying him his favorite cookies?

"Well, you know they're better once they've had a minute to set," she said in an excited voice. "Plus, these are for the little miss upstairs. I imagine she'll be hungry, and dinner won't be ready for a few hours yet. It's so nice to finally have a lady in the house!"

He didn't bother to ask how Molly knew Halle was upstairs. Between the two brownies, they knew *everything* that happened in this house, and he'd accepted that about their particular magic years ago. Viktor couldn't help but frown. Already this female was causing strife in his household, and she hadn't even been here for a full hour. He knew he should take her somewhere else immediately before his peace and quiet were gone for good … not to mention his cookies, but just the thought of having her out of his immediate reach stirred uncomfortable feelings in his chest that he decided to ignore.

Molly had tried to play matchmaker the first couple of decades when they'd come on staff, thinking that Viktor needed a woman in his life, but he'd quickly expressed his displeasure in her efforts and she'd let it go. The last thing he wanted now was for her to get her hopes up that Halle would be here for longer than necessary and start all that shit up again.

"She isn't staying. This is just temporary until we find her somewhere safe to go," he said as he used his vampire reflexes to snatch a cookie off the tray and continue on his way into the study.

"Sure it is, ya rascal," Molly said, laughing after him, "I saw the befuddled look on your face when you came down the stairs. This one will be different."

Viktor could've sworn he heard a ghostly snickering laugh that sounded suspiciously like the little goth fairy from the bar as he left the kitchen and entered his study, but his senses told him there was no one there…

Well—that was creepy. Maybe it is time to get the house exorcised?

Chapter Seven

"Pandora, what are you doing?"

"Sweet baby Lucifer!" Dori screamed and jumped as her bedroom door flew the rest of the way open to admit one of the scariest beings she had ever known. "You scared the crap outta me, Nana. What the hell?"

"Your mom called me again, Missy, and she told me that you've been using a lot of magic lately." The tiny fairy stormed into Dori's room in her four-inch heels and pastel pink Chanel suit ensemble.

Her nana looked pointedly at the remote viewing crystal ball Dori had been watching closely. "More like wasting magic as I can see it! Why can't you just watch HBO like the rest of us when you want a little drama, girl? I've told you over and over, magic isn't a never-ending resource. The energy you use to create it comes from somewhere, and there is always a toll on the user. Your mother is terrified that you will up and fade away one day if you're not more careful!"

"Nana, I'm not watching TV. I'm keeping tabs on my clients to see how they're progressing," Dori said as she closed the view screen, but not before her Nana got a good look at the handsome vampire through it … and by the flare of her sparkly green wings, she recognized him.

"Was that Viktor *The Destroyer* you were spying on?"

"I'm not *spying,* per se. You make it sound like I'm some creepy pervert with a sharp tooth fetish, Nan, Gods."

"Wait—you said, 'client'. Please tell me you haven't been selling your charms to the beasts and undesirables down at The Pit again. Goddess help me, Barbara from my bridge club will never let me live this down!" her nana wailed throwing her hands up in a dramatic fashion that only Dori's grandmother could pull off.

"Good grief, Nana, could you be any more dramatic?" Dori matched her with her own eye roll and hand gestures. "If you *must* know, I've started a new business. I'm finding Happy Ever Afters for those who are too much of a challenge for the *non-talented* Fairy Godmothers. You know I've got the skills, so I've just decided to use them for the greater good just like you and Mom are always droning on and on about and all that crap."

Dori really thought that her declaration would have made her Nana happy, even dare she say … proud? But inexplicably, an even more devastated look took up residence on her grandmother's magically non-wrinkled face.

"You've gone *rogue*?! Oy vey! What have I done in a past life to deserve such a horrible grandchild? I'm going to get *kicked out* of my bridge club once this gets out!" she cried out once again throwing her hands in the air.

"First of all, Nan, we're not Jewish, so you can just can it with the guilt trip. Second, I haven't gone rogue. I'm not poaching names from the official listing of Happy Ever Afters. I'm simply reevaluating those who may have been rejected or overlooked due to some behavioral issues in their past." Dori tried to explain to her Nana what she was too afraid to tell her mother when she decided to start her new venture. Her poor mom had been judged enough in her life because of Pandora. What she didn't know now, Pandora hoped, wouldn't hurt her.

That news, once it sank in, had her nana's waterworks drying up quickly, the switch was so immediate Dori couldn't help but be impressed.

Obviously, her own exceptional "people management skills" must have come straight from her grandmother.

"Hold on, are you telling me that you're using your vast magical abilities to find Happy Ever Afters for … villains?"

The look on her nana's face said it all. Sure, it was half confusion, but the other half was as though she'd just stepped in the biggest, foulest pile of dog shit ever.

"You know, Nana, you're such an elitist. Most of these so-called *villains* are simply different and misunderstood, just like me. It's about time that someone helped them for a change, instead of all of you having your heads crammed so far up 'Prince Charming's' ass that you can see his tonsils!" Dori ranted as she heard her mom finally wander upstairs to see what all the noise was about.

"What's going on up here with all the yelling? Belinda down the street just called and asked if my daughter had finally gone full 'Vader' on me and if she should call the enforcers to come and put you down!" her mom said as she stood at the doorway to her room.

Pandora couldn't help but snort out a laugh. *Oh that Belinda, she is such a funny old bitch.* Dori made a mental note to send her an anonymous bouquet of stink-weed in a Darth Vader mug. *Good luck getting that stank outta your drapes, you old cow!*

"Do you know that your daughter is finding Happy Ever Afters for criminals and villains, Tabitha?" her Nana blurted out before Dori could break it gently to her mom.

All three of them were silent for a few moments after her Nana so rudely outed her to the only person in the world whose opinion actually mattered to Dori. She was almost afraid to look at her mom's face, terrified at the disappointment she might see there.

"Is this true, Pandora?" her mom questioned in a quiet voice.

Dammit, Tabitha Bellor was the only being on this planet that Dori wouldn't lie to.

"Yes." she sighed back.

"Why?"

Huh? Her mother had found out what she'd been doing with her magic and there was no immediate yelling and grounding? That was a first.

"Because—I don't know, it just came to me one day that there was no reason why all of those beings without a 'perfect record of goodness' didn't deserve a chance to be happy just the same as all those pansy-ass do-gooders on the Grand Fairies stupid listing. People aren't supposed to be perfect you know. That doesn't mean that they don't deserve happiness, too!"

Dori didn't want to admit to her mother or grandmother that one of the reasons she was so passionate about this, was that she herself would not be eligible for a Happy Ending according to Fairy Godmother law. Her dark wings had marked her from birth that she wasn't like the rest of them. But that didn't make her evil. Sure she had a tendency to find more trouble than most fairies, but a girl had to have *some* fun, right?

"Dori, look at me," her mother said as Dori refused to make eye contact after her rant.

Finally, with a sigh, she looked at her mother and was surprised to see a gentle smile on her face.

"I'm so proud of you, Pandora," her mother said.

"What?"

"What!"

The matching outbursts came from Pandora and her grandmother both.

"You've finally found your purpose, my dear," Tabitha said as she walked over and gathered her daughter in a tight hug. "I always knew that you would be destined for great things, and I agree with you. Everyone deserves a chance at a Happy Ending, and it's about time that someone finally came along with the power to make it happen."

Pandora hugged her mom back. She was so incredibly happy that someone else understood what she had only stumbled upon by instinct. She felt a small amount of shame that she hadn't trusted in her mother all this time. After all, Tabitha had believed in her even before she was born.

"What if I suck at it?" Dori whispered her doubts out loud for the first time since this whole idea had taken root inside of her.

"Impossible!" Her mother laughed and looked down at her. "Who could be better at manipulating people than you are, love?"

It felt so good to laugh along with her mother, with everything out on the table now. It was like a giant weight had been lifted off of her wings.

"Oh, I don't know, I think Nana could give me a run for my money."

Even her crotchety old grandmother couldn't help but laugh at that.

"Now come down to the kitchen and tell us all about your first clients, baby. I want to hear everything!" her mother said as she tugged Pandora out of her room and down the hall to where the smell of her mother's homemade double chocolate chip cookies was beckoning. Not even Nana's cranky disposition could fight the double chocolate chip.

Chapter Eight

Two plates of cookies and a whole pot of coffee later, a minor miracle had occurred. Both Dori's mother *and* her Nana had to admit once they'd heard Viktor's story, that he did indeed deserve a chance at a Happy Ever After. Although, when her mother asked her how Dori had known before she'd researched him, she didn't have an answer to give.

Deep down inside of her, she just instinctually knew whether or not someone deserved a Happy Ending. Which was rather unheard of in the Fairy Godmother world. It may look all "bibbity, bobbity, boo", but a shit-ton of hours went into the background checks and a full history of every applicant on the Grand Fairy's master name list.

In fact, around seventy-five percent of all graduating Fairy Godmothers or -fathers were relegated to the research office, and only twenty-five percent ever made it to a coveted field position. Dori also speculated that it was those exact same statistics which were responsible for the reason that more time wasn't taken to sort out the most complicated cases such as Viktor's.

It took more than arranging a smokin' hot dress, pair of glass slippers, and a ride to the ball to ensure that folks like Viktor and Halle would get the chance they deserved. Quite frankly, the run-of-the-mill Fairy Godmother simply just didn't have the magical chops to pull off that kind of magic.

Dori liked to think of herself as a black rose within a field of weedy under-achievers.

By the end of the afternoon, Dori's mother was bound and determined to help in any way she could. Her mom always was a sucker for a love story after all, but it wasn't a huge surprise that her Nana was holding out, no doubt waiting to see if Dori would fall flat on her face.

"You can't tell anyone about this. You know the council wouldn't understand what I'm trying to do," Dori warned as the little old lady looked slightly affronted that she'd even mention it. "Snitches get stitches, Nana."

"Ha! Like I would knowingly spread around my own social demise. What am I, some kind of ninnyhammer?" Nana said once again throwing her hands up in the air. "I swear you two will be the end of me with your blatant disregard for our Fairy Godmother way of life. Our lineage comes from Fairy royalty you know!"

"We know," Dori and her mom said in unison, Goddess help them if she went on *that* rant again.

Well, at least she had her mom's support in all this. Who knows? If she could actually pull this first job off, maybe the old bat would change her tune?

Dori decided that it was high time to get back to her current clients and help her sweet little Halle-cat get the cream.

****

"Wow, this place is impressive!" Dori said as she popped into the lush, expensive bathroom behind Halle.

"Ah! What the hell, Dori? You scared the crap out of me!" Halle screamed and jumped about three feet straight up in the air in a very feline-like move.

"Huh, well that's creepy," Dori said after staring for a second. "Try not to do that jumping thing in front of Viktor until we lock this down, okay?"

"Whatever. Hey, can you 'hocus pocus' me in some clothes or something? I'm covered in blood spatter, and I'd rather not put these back on," Halle said, as she leaned into the enormous stone shower and turned on the water.

"Hmm, I have just the thing!" Dori said, before

she popped back out of the room in a wink of magic, then seconds later reappeared with a man's shirt in her hands.

"Not that I'm not grateful or anything, but couldn't you have grabbed me some yoga pants and a sweatshirt?" Halle eyed the way too large, men's striped dress shirt—which just happened to smell deliciously like her host.

"Nope," Dori said, shaking her head while she tapped her finger on an imaginary wristwatch. "We're on a seduction timeline here, Halle, and I think you'll find Viktor's reaction to you wearing his shirt will be very favorable."

"Fine," Halle sighed in defeat. "At least my underwear is still clean so I'll just put them back on."

"Double nope," Dori replied with an evil smirk before she vanished into thin air.

Halle squealed as she felt a weird tickling of magic under her clothes the same moment that Dori left.

What the hell was that? She undid her pants and slipped them off along with her shirt.

She was shocked when she realized that both her bra and panties had magically disappeared.

"Freakin' fairies…" she grumbled as she stepped into the hot shower.

The water felt so amazing after the crap day that Halle had had so far. There was a rain shower head and six more nozzles on the walls of the stone monstrosity. She could have stayed inside for hours letting the hot water drown her stress.

Finally, once she was good and pruney, she reluctantly turned off the taps and stepped out to dry off and try to get dressed for seduction … whatever *that* meant. Halle wiped the steam off of the large vanity mirror with her hand and took a hard look at the woman staring back. The shirt Dori had given her was large enough that it went to mid-thigh, and she'd rolled the sleeves up. Her hair was towel dried and looking cute in a tousled kind of way.

I can totally do this. I can seduce a reportedly vicious vampire and convince him to keep me forever ... right?

Ok, she was way out of her depth, but the fairy said this was her one chance to keep her mate and she was going to give it everything she had. That settled, she took a deep breath, undid the top three buttons on the shirt, turned and made her way downstairs to confront her future—and, she hoped, make out with it a little.

Chapter Nine

Viktor heard the little patter of Halle's bare feet as she came down the stairs. Truth be told, he'd been so distracted imagining her in the shower he didn't even know how long he'd been standing in front of the fire in his study. He had no idea what in the hell had gotten into him. Even when he'd met his wife all those years ago, he hadn't remembered having such an obsessive reaction to a female.

However, nothing could have prepared him for the sight that met his eyes when Halle came around the corner. There she stood, fresh and warm from her shower, her blonde locks framing her face in soft layers.

Sweet Goddess.

She was wearing one of his button-down shirts, the top open enough to show a delicious tease of her ample cleavage. His cock quickly went from half hard, to "trying to break out of his pants to reach her" and he had to adjust his stance quickly to try to hide that fact. His eyes roamed over her bare legs. They certainly were long and toned for such a tiny little thing. Her shifter genes were apparent in the perfection of her curvy form. Viktor could hear the increase in her heartbeat as she got closer to him. Naturally, he assumed it was nerves or fear, but when she stepped closer and he picked up her scent, it was the sweet aroma of heat and arousal that teased his nose.

Now there was really no hiding what she did to his body. He'd never been so hard in all his life. Her eyes dropped to the large outline of his cock through his pants, and the scent of her honey increased, drawing a low moan from his mouth when her pink tongue darted out to lick her lips. Now he was fully imagining those plump lips wrapped around his dick and if he didn't distract himself soon he would lose control.

No, I brought this woman into my home to protect her from Conrad, and I would be just as bad if I jumped on her myself.

Clearing his throat, he took a step back from the temptation in front of him. After all, Viktor was nothing if not in control of his baser urges. He still held much regret from his actions when he was first turned and there was nothing worse in this world than regrets. They were always there … haunting you.

"Dinner will be ready in an hour or so. Would you like a tour of the house? I have quite an extensive art collection," he said with a tense smile, offering her his arm to escort her.

****

Halle had seen the desire on his face when she walked into the room, and it was impossible to miss the enormous bulge in the front of his pants that confirmed his interest. So why the most feared and reputed villain of the entire paranormal community was acting like a perfect gentleman was baffling to her.

Dori had told her repeatedly that Viktor really wasn't the man his reputation painted him to be, but in the back of her mind, Halle had expected a lot of habits and behavior that she'd have to either try to change or accept about this man she didn't know, if she went through with this plan.

Especially if they were indeed mates. Her leopard paced inside of her head impatiently, implying there was no doubt in *its* mind that Viktor was their mate. The cat wanted to pounce on him immediately and never let him go, no matter what people said about him. Her animal half was proud that their mate was a fierce fighter and would be strong enough to protect their young. That was all that was important to her.

When it came to fated mates, shifters were a simple bunch. If your beast told you that someone was your mate, then that person was *it*. Whether your human half liked them at the time or not. So there was always the possibility that fate would give you the shaft and mate you to someone who was a complete dick. Hope began to blossom in her that Viktor was something more than the monster in the stories told to frighten young para children.

She looped her arm through his, her cat itching to get that much closer. When she stepped into him and the side of her breast brushed against his arm she felt his muscles tense.

"I'd love for you to take me," she said in a low purr.

"What?" he answered, startled, his eyes growing wide.

"On a tour of the house? Like you just said?" Halle answered, blinking innocent big green eyes up at him with a small smile.

Oh dear. This is going to be way too much fun. Halle all of a sudden felt the full force of her feminine wiles for the first time ever, and the brat inside of her was gleefully rubbing her hands together imagining ways to tease the handsome vampire.

"Oh ... of course," he answered, looking a bit suspicious of her big kitty cat eyes. "We'll start in the great room."

Halle delighted in tormenting Viktor throughout the entire house tour. She would step in close to him to get a better look at certain paintings, touching him whenever possible and absently playing with the buttons on the shirt she was wearing. It was probably the most fun she'd ever had in her life, but teasing was a double-edged sword. The more aroused Viktor became, the more she wanted him in return. By the time he ended their house tour she could see his fangs had fully extended and hers were aching to answer in kind.

The only problem now? She had no idea how to take things to the next level, being the virgin that she was, and her stubborn vamp seemed determined to resist their attraction. While her cat was telling her to pounce on what was theirs, she wasn't sure she had the balls to do it.

Chapter Ten

By all the Gods, this woman is trying to drive me mad!

Viktor could clearly see that Halle was enjoying teasing him and any other man would've just taken her up against the nearest wall by now, but there was just something about her that drove his protective instincts to a place they hadn't gone in an eternity, not since his wife and son had been alive.

That thought in itself should've been enough to have him running the other way. He'd been alone for so long that the idea of having someone to actually care about again was terrifying. He had made so many enemies over the years, and the last thing he ever wanted to do was to give them a weakness to exploit. He also never wanted to feel the kind of loss again that came with taking a chance on loving someone, only to be disappointed by fate.

No. He would endure this torture and leave her be. A nice girl like Halle deserved a nice, simple life, with a mate and children. All he had to do was resist the temptation for a few days until he found her somewhere safe to hide out, and then he would finally go and deal with Conrad himself. That bastard would no longer be playing games with innocent peoples' lives. That would be his gift to Halle.

****

Dori sat in the living room of her mom's place in front of the viewing crystal with a big bowl of popcorn and a frown on her face.

It had been *days* of Halle flirting her ass off and leaving subtle innuendos for Viktor to take advantage of. The truth was, Dori was damned proud of her girl. For someone who had little to no dating history, she was going at that man like the classiest of call girls, strutting her stuff all over that house. But the male was the most stubborn ass Dori had ever encountered. Of course, being the enlightened individual she was, she knew that he was resisting Halle out of some sense of honor and protection towards the girl, which only made him more likable—*if* you were into that kind of thing.

Damned honorable males, how dare he mess with my timetable!

Dori knew that Halle's fragile sense of feminine pride could only last so long when she was getting rebuffed left and right. She'd put money on the fact that the little shifter would have already beat feet home if her cat hadn't confirmed that Viktor was indeed her true mate—even if that would have meant ending up dealing with Conrad on her own or not.

But luckily for all of them, now that Halle's cat had scented her mate, the tenacious little beastie wouldn't accept *no* for an answer.

So, how would they break this surprisingly chivalrous villain's rock hard control? Well, since the subtle sexual invitation wasn't working, Dori had to reach back into her bag of tricks for motivating the opposite sex, and she was pretty sure she'd found the perfect thing.

As soon as she watched Viktor excused himself out of the study to go make a call and see if Gerald was making any progress with Halle's relocation, Dori popped into sight beside Halle.

"Goddess, Dori! You scared the crap out of me again," Halle whispered furiously. "It's been days, and this isn't working. I'm not sure I can do this."

Dori felt the oddest uncomfortable flutter in her chest region as she watched Halle's lower lip quiver and her eyes begin to well up with tears. She could have sworn she almost felt the need to hug her—she must have been PMS'ing or something as she certainly wasn't one of those "touchy feely" fairies.

"Shh, of course, you can, pet. Halle, look at me." She waited until she had Halle's undivided attention as she was about to drop some tough love on the perky little shifter. "Why should the Universe, or why should *I* for that matter, fight for your Happy Ending if you aren't willing to do the same? This shit is tough, and true love can be a vicious bitch sometimes, but you need to suck it up. Consider those tears a down payment on your Happy Ever After."

Halle took a minute to no doubt absorb the invaluable lesson that she'd just given her. The girl wiped at her huge green eyes, and when they flashed in defiance Dori knew she was ready for another crack at it.

"Viktor is just trying to do what he thinks is best for you, but I know exactly what will break him."

"What?"

"Bare ass and a challenge, my girl. He's got a solid lock on his self-control against your flirting, but if you flash a little more skin and then challenge his manhood? Well, honey, I haven't met an alpha male yet who will let that invitation go. Plus—the sex will be super-hot," she said with a wink right before she left in a poof of magic.

****

Pandora arrived home and almost landed on top of her mother in the living room, now eating *her* bowl of popcorn.

"Hey, that's mine. I busted my ass putting that in the microwave!" she said as she snatched the bowl away with a hoot of victory.

"Honestly, darling, no wonder there's a rumor going around that you were raised by demon wolves."

They both settled in on the couch in front of the viewing crystal to see if Halle would take her advice. When the little shifter got a determined look on her face and ran upstairs to change into another one of Viktor's shirts that she'd pilfered, Dori knew the fireworks were about to commence.

"Ooh, she's going for it." Her mother squealed in delight and clapped her hands. "Honestly, this is so much more exciting than reality TV!"

"This better work because they're running out of time," Dori said as she felt that tingling of her magic deep down in her chest. She closed her eyes and quickly checked on the internal timeline she had for Viktor and Halle.

"What in the hell was that?" her mom asked, with a freaked-out tone in her voice.

"What?" Dori said in a distracted voice, and when she opened her eyes again her mother was staring over her shoulder at her wings like she'd never seen them before.

"What were you just doing? Your wings were glowing and vibrating. I've never heard of fairy wings *ever* doing that."

Glowing and vibrating? Dori had no idea there were physical manifestations when she used the deepest of her magic, but then again, she'd never done it in front of anyone before. One of these days, Pandora was going to have to push her mom to tell her more about who her father was. She still had no idea who or *what* he had been.

Every time she brought it up, her mom quickly shut the conversation down. But things were getting weird, and maybe if she knew what kind of power her father had possessed, she'd be able to master her own magic better. That and maybe her mother could stop worrying that she'd burn out and fade away every time Dori got lazy and manifested a Starbucks latte instead of driving to the mall.

Chapter Eleven

Four days went by, and Viktor was beginning to worry that his self-control wouldn't hold out much longer. Gerald and Molly still hadn't found a safe haven to stash Halle that Conrad's goons didn't have access to. It seemed as though the Coven Master wanted her back something fierce, as he'd spared no expense in bribing all manner of beings to be on the lookout for the runaway leopard shifter. Conrad had put a five-million-dollar bounty out on each of them, and while Halle's was extremely specific about her being intact and unharmed, the price on Viktor's head was dead or alive.

How touching.

Regardless, it had meant that the last four days had been spent in close quarters, neither of them able to leave the safety of his warded home. Molly had brought some clothes for Halle to wear, but the vexing female still spent most of her time looking delectable in *his* shirts, and though he had no proof, in his mind she wore nothing else underneath. They spent their time playing games, reading and watching movies, but he could see that her inner cat was beginning to get twitchy to go for a run. He'd caught her more than once standing in front of the large window in the library, staring longingly at the woods behind the house. Viktor couldn't stop himself from sending Gerald to the witches to purchase extended warding that would protect the forest behind them. It would cost him a small fortune, but something in him needed to take care of this woman, no matter the cost.

Halle had fallen in love with his library, and they sat and talked for hours about their favorite books, but she was constantly touching him and flirting with him. In a bid to distract himself from her physically, he decided he'd have to do something he normally didn't do since she'd already told him so much about her own life. He'd have to talk to her about *himself.*

"So," he began as he settled himself in the chair beside her, "you'd said that you have an older brother. Is he mated yet?"

"Nah, Tavin is a hopeless romantic, much to my dad's frustration." She smiled as she spoke of her brother, and it was clear she was quite fond of him. "He refuses to mate any females in the pard, or anyone else my parents have suggested. He's convinced that the perfect woman is out there, just waiting for him."

"And how about you?" he asked softly. "Do you believe in the perfect mating?"

Halle paused for a moment, and this was the first time that Viktor got the feeling that she was censoring her thoughts with him, and he didn't care for it at all. He wanted to know exactly what she was thinking and feeling. Perhaps it would make him feel less confused about the nature of his own odd feelings since she had arrived in his life.

"I think I do," she finally answered. "I mean, I know a lot of people get lonely and settle for someone who they think they can love, or that they know will be a good partner. But I'd rather be alone than not be with the one who makes my heart sing. My cat will settle for nothing less."

"I was married once, before I was turned," he said quietly, not making eye contact with Halle. He was scared at what her face would reveal in regard to his news. If she was jealous, then it would seem his attraction was reciprocated and he would have no more excuses to fight it. Even worse, if she didn't seem to care at all, he was afraid the disappointment would crush him.

So much for not letting anyone in.
"Oh."

Viktor silently thanked the gods when he dared a peek and saw the spark of anger that lit up her shifter's eyes before she got her emotions under control.

"What happened to her … after—after you turned?"

He knew in his head he would have to tell her the story of his turning when he'd opened this line of conversation, but thinking it and telling it were two very different things. Would she judge him and hate him after this, just like everyone else did?

"I was plucked from the battlefield and kept for many years as a blood slave by my creator. When she finally feared that I was getting too old to keep her sexual interest, she turned me. I had endured so many horrors within the coven and my hatred had grown so much, that as soon as I'd woken in my new life I destroyed her and her people in my bloodlust and anger."

"Did you go back for your family?"

"I had become the monster every mortal feared." He finally looked up and was surprised to see the tenderness in her face. "I couldn't risk harming them, and things were so different back then. My wife had been told I'd been killed in battle, and she had remarried to provide for our son."

"That must have hurt you."

"I could not blame her for it." Viktor hadn't thought about his wife Lelaina for centuries. It had been so long since both she and his son had passed. "The Roman empire was a harsh place for a woman without the protection of a strong man. We had married young, just like most did. I was fond of Lelaina and I loved my son, but I was content they would be taken care of in my absence."

"I can understand that I guess."

"I was filled with such rage that I was unable to

control, I spent years tracking the last of Melisandre's coven. I was unfit to be around any living being, especially mortals."

He couldn't hide the shame in his confession.

"Of course you were enraged. It was awful what was done to you, Viktor. What was taken from you could never be forgiven." Halle reached out and placed her hand on his arm, causing him to look up at her once again.

"Do not mistake me, Halle." His pride was pushing him to tell her everything, whether it was self-sabotaging or not. "I've done all the horrible things in my life that others whisper about me. Terrible, unforgivable things. My soul will never be rid of their taint."

She just stared into his eyes, her stubbornness matching his own.

"The fact that you just told me that shows me exactly what type of man you are now Viktor. No one is without sin, but it's how you choose to live your life now and the man you've become that matters to me."

He was stunned at her words. Deep inside Viktor had been certain that confessing his past to Halle would be the thing that had her fleeing him in disgust. How did she have so much faith in him? He'd spent so many years believing he had no future, that his sins had condemned him, that when he was presented with the possibility of one—he'd been left speechless.

Chapter Twelve

Thank the Gods for Gerald's impeccable timing.

"Sir, the warding at the back of the property has been completed as per your request," the brownie said as he stood in the entry to the library with a curious gaze towards them. "Miss Halle is safe now to shift and run in the woods."

Halle's eyes immediately left the small man who'd interrupted them and zeroed in back on Viktor.

"You did that for me?" she asked as a huge smile lit up her face, and suddenly Viktor would have paid any price those criminal witches had asked. He'd give his entire fortune up to make this woman smile like that at him.

All he could do was nod at her like a complete and utter moron.

"Can I go now?"

When he nodded once again, she jumped up in a squeal and ran for the veranda doors as she began to undress.

Viktor just stood and stared off after Halle as her bare golden skin bounced along in the sun. Finally, Gerald's throat clearing got his attention and he looked towards the brownie, who was now motioning him out the door.

"Perhaps you should follow and make sure she's *safe*?" His bushy eyebrows moved up and down to exaggerate his point.

"Oh yes," Viktor agreed as he quickly strode out onto the patio just in time to see her shift seamlessly into a beautiful, graceful leopard … and then roll in the grass like she was a golden retriever.

He almost laughed at the ridiculously content expression that was on her kitty face by the time he'd walked over to her. She was purring loudly and walked over to butt her head up against his leg.

"You can run in the woods, Halle. Just don't roam too far," he said as he stroked her silky fur and scratched behind her ears before she bolted away from him into the tree line.

He gathered her discarded clothing and folded it, then sat in a chair on the patio, using his vampire hearing to keep track of her as she played in the trees and the brush. Viktor was still amazed at how easy it was to open up to her. He'd talked more about his life to Halle in the last four days than he'd shared with anyone in over a thousand years. The woman certainly did like to talk. But the most difficult thing had been the constant arousal that he had to deal with every time he looked at her, or smelled her, or heard her voice. Each night he had lain in bed imagining her in the next room while he stroked himself to ease the pressure. But as soon as he'd come, all it would take was a sniff of her scent or the sound of her voice and his cock was ready for her again. It was madness, and her teasing and flirting were wearing him down.

When she finally lollygagged out of the forest an hour later, he could tell she had enjoyed herself. She stopped right in front of him and shifted back into her skin, complete with a sexy, bold smile that she hadn't given him before. Viktor just stood there, taking the beauty of her in. He wanted her to see the appreciation in his gaze before he handed her clothes back to her.

"That was wonderful, thank you, Viktor," she said as she dressed. Her voice was huskier than normal, and he wondered if the rumors about shifters being aroused after they changed forms were true. She smelled beyond amazing with the wild scent of the wind and the earth clinging to her skin, and it was all he could do to take a step back and escort her back through the library doors without touching her.

Viktor had a lot of thinking to do.

He decided to do it alone in his office while Halle was upstairs cleaning up, but hard as he tried, he couldn't get the radiant sight of all that bare golden skin out of his head.

This is ridiculous! I am acting like a hormonal teenager.

The bottom line was that Halle would be a weakness his enemies could exploit. She could get hurt. He'd be a fool to get involved with her—no matter how good she smelled.

It's settled then. I'll simply keep my distance until I find her somewhere to go.

Viktor had heard Halle's little feet come back down the stairs a few minutes ago, so he went back to the library as that's where she spent almost all of her time. He looked up as he walked through the entryway to the large room and had to do a double-take when he saw Halle halfway up the ladder at the bookshelves, her bare thighs peeking out from beneath his shirt once more. He shifted his stance as his cock filled and his imagination began to run wild with all the things he wanted to do to her. When Halle looked back over her shoulder and a small seductive smile crept over her lips when she saw where his gaze was riveted to, his control finally snapped.

"What are you playing at here, Halle?" he said, as he watched her climb back down the ladder and he went to the bar to fix a drink. "Are you looking for someone to scratch an itch? I'm not exactly the kind of man your type usually looks for."

He regretted his words instantly as the look of desire on her face quickly turned into hurt, and then anger.

"You asshole!" she spat back at him. "You want me just as much as I want you. Do you think I go around throwing myself at just any man? Dori said you'd be stubborn, but this is ridiculous."

"Dori? That crazy fairy from the bar?" he asked suspiciously, "What does she have to do with you trying to seduce me? Is this some kind of spell?"

That at least would explain the odd protective feelings and his overwhelming need to touch Halle, but what would a random fairy have against him?

"No, this isn't a spell, you idiot!" Halle seemed furious now that he would accuse her of doing something so vile and needy. "You're lucky I'm even *considering* having sex with someone like you!"

That statement flared up his temper and along with it, the last shreds of his self-control disappeared. Before she could blink he had her pinned against the wall, his left hand wrapped around her wrists, holding them above her head. There was a second of panic in her eyes before he felt her muscles relax beneath him.

"*Considering* it, kitten?" he whispered low in her ear as he leaned in close. "I could've had you bent over every piece of furniture in my house a dozen times over in the last five days if I'd wanted and you would've loved every second of it."

Chapter Thirteen

He could feel her pulse beat wildly at that statement, and by the sweet scent coming from between her shapely legs, Viktor was pleasantly surprised that she seemed to be even more turned on by his dominance. But she wasn't quite ready to submit to him yet. He saw her swallow hard and try to get her breathing under control.

"I think you just talk a big game," she answered back in a low voice. "You've jumped every time I touched you."

Saucy little minx. She was still challenging him, was she? Perhaps it was time to give her what she was looking for, to hell with him trying to do the right thing.

"Well, then let me grant you your wish … although you may get more than you bargained for, little one," Viktor said as he took his free hand and slowly trailed his palm up along the outside of her thigh.

He had to hide his delighted surprise and stifle a groan when he got to her hip under the shirt and found that she wasn't wearing any underwear. He let his fingers tickle lightly across the skin at the top of her pelvis, knowing it was driving her crazy. He could already feel the increased heat coming from her pussy and knew she would be soaking wet when he finally reached his goal.

"My, my, aren't you full of surprises, kitten. If I'd known you weren't wearing any underwear this entire time, I would've abandoned the pleasantries to have a taste of this delicious little puss days ago," he said, right before he closed the space between their mouths and kissed her hard and deep.

Viktor was lost at the first taste of her in his mouth. She kissed him back with just as much passion, and he knew that this was going to be a wild ride. His cock was already leaking at the thought of sliding inside her wet heat, but he wasn't going to last long this first time, and he wanted a taste of her honey before that happened. He released her wrists and picked her up with a firm grip on her generous ass. He couldn't wait to feel it cushion him as he fucked her hard from behind. Curves like hers were made for a man to enjoy.

One hard push had the chess board on the table in front of the fireplace tumbling to the ground, and he gently laid her down in its place. He met her eyes as he took her shirttails in his fingers and tore the garment open, leaving her golden, tanned skin bare to his hungry gaze. The contrast of his pale hands against her skin was mesmerizing. She was utter perfection. Her hair spread wildly against the dark table top. She was biting her lip as his hands reached up to palm her breasts. They fit his hands perfectly, and when he softly rolled her nipples between his fingers, the moan that came out of her was music to his ears.

"Gods, Halle, you're so perfect," he said, moving his hands slowly down her stomach to the bounty awaiting him below. "You smell so fucking good. I can't wait to get my mouth on you."

"Yes, Viktor, oh my God, I need you to touch me," Halle moaned out as he pushed her thighs open wide, exposing her to his gaze.

"Mmm, where do you want me to touch you, baby?" he asked as he lowered himself to his knees in front of her. "Do you want me to lick this wet little pussy?"

Viktor had never seen anything so fucking hot in all his lifetime. Her mound was bare, already swollen and glistening for him.

"Yes, please lick me."

The first swipe of his tongue along her wet folds had both of them moaning.

Gods, she tastes so fucking good. That was the thought that kept on playing over and over in his head.

He was certain he could eat her out for days at a time and never be satisfied. He ran his tongue all along the length of her pussy, sucking on her lips until finally, he trailed the tip of his tongue up to circle her swollen clit. He heard her nails dig into the wood of the table and took that as a compliment. Viktor hadn't taken a lot of lovers over the years, but when he did he'd made a point to make sure that they were well satisfied. He latched onto the little bud and suckled hard as he pushed two fingers deep inside her. She was so tight, and so hot around his flesh, he could've sworn he felt some resistance, but when Halle screamed and came around his fingers, his thoughts became all about getting his cock inside of her as quickly as possible. He gave her clit one more slow draw and felt her flutter around his buried digits once again as he slowly worked his fingers inside of her.

The look on her face when she opened her beautiful green eyes and locked with his almost took his breath away.

"Viktor, I need you inside of me," she said, her fangs now fully extended in her mouth.

Viktor had never slept with a shifter before, but damn if seeing her dainty little fangs in her mouth didn't turn him on. He'd been careful not to let her feel his own while he'd gone down on her, but as he looked into the heated depths of her eyes he let the tip of one canine drag lightly across her clit and almost came in his pants as she panted "Fuck, oh God, that's going to make me come again."

"Next time you come, it's going to be on my cock," he said as he stood up and quickly tore at his shirt and pants.

Chapter Fourteen

He loved the way her eyes widened as his shirt hit the floor, and when he opened his pants and pushed them down his hips, he had to grab the base of his cock just to keep from embarrassing himself when she licked her lips and stared at his dick like she wanted to devour it.

"Wow," she said quietly. "Viktor, you're beautiful."

Viktor actually felt himself blush at her genuine appreciation. He couldn't remember the last time anyone had looked at him like that.

"No, baby, you're the stunning one." His hand slowly stroked along his shaft, and her eyes clouded over with lust again.

When he stepped back up to her and ran the aching, swollen head of his cock along her soaking folds, his eyes closed at how good it felt. He couldn't have stopped the groan that left his lips even if he wanted to.

"Oh wow, that feels amazing," she said in a breathless voice as her hips moved under him.

Over and over again, he rubbed along her pussy, teasing them both. When he took the tip of his dick and tapped it over her clit, she almost came right off the table.

"Oh God, Viktor, do that again," she moaned, grasping at the edges of the tabletop.

This time, he took his shaft in hand and gave her a hard smack against her wet pussy and she did come, screaming his name. Viktor then took the fat head of his cock and fit it against her opening, and pushed in with one long thrust.

Holy fuck, is she tight, he thought to himself as he tried to keep from losing control.

He felt her entire body tense up and stopped

moving immediately when a tiny whimper escaped her mouth.

"What's wrong, Halle? Did I hurt you?" he asked in a panic, not moving a muscle.

"You're just a bit bigger than I thought, that's all," she said through gritted teeth. "Just give me a minute."

"You're really tight. Has it been a while for you, love?" He moved his hands up to cup and massaged her breasts, trying to help her relax.

"Umm, well … I've never really done this before," she said quietly, as she looked at the fire, trying to avoid his eyes.

Viktor was shocked.

Halle was a virgin, and she hadn't even said anything to me?

The animalistic part of him was ridiculously pleased that he'd been the first to claim her sweet body, but the rest of him was concerned that he'd hurt her and irritated that she hadn't been up front with him. Back when he'd still been a human, you didn't just take a woman's virginity. In those times, that was the fastest way to get yourself a trip to a priest and a new wife— either that or you would find yourself run through at the end of her father's sword.

Of course, logically he knew that times had changed. Sexuality was something that was celebrated and not shamed in this time. However, he couldn't help but wonder why a beautiful woman her age would still be a virgin.

"Why didn't you tell me, Halle?" he asked, as he slowly started to back out of her. "I could've hurt you."

"No!" she said in a panic, gripping her legs around his ass stopping his retreat. "Don't stop, I'm fine now. Please, Viktor."

He swallowed hard at the feel of her sheath relaxing and flexing around him.

Gods, it feels good. He was having a hard time remembering the reason that he felt they should stop. After all, the damage was done now.

I may as well make her first time a memorable one, right? That would be the gentlemanly thing to do—not that he was a gentleman.

"Ok, but tell me if you feel any pain," he said, slowly moving forward again, "and don't think we won't be talking about this later."

"Fine, later," she said breathlessly, as her hips started to move against him.

When he was finally all the way back inside of her, his balls resting against her ass, he leaned forward and took her lips in a slow and thorough kiss. Viktor ate at her mouth like he was a starving man. He could feel her pussy getting wetter and wetter around him, and then she finally pulled her lips a fraction away from his and whispered the magic words.

"I need you to fuck me now, Viktor."

Viktor lost all the hard-won control he had. Thank the Gods for a shifter's faster healing abilities. He pulled out of her and pushed back in fast, loving how wet and hot she was on his dick. No woman had ever felt as good as she did. He tried to temper his thrusts, not wanting to be too rough, but when her little cat claws dug into the cheeks of his ass and her murmurs of *faster and harder* reached his ears, he was relieved to give her what they both needed.

He pounded into her, grinding into her swollen clit with each thrust, and when he felt her pussy start to grip him tight, he pushed as deep inside of her as he could get before he came and groaned out her name. At that same moment, she pulled his head up to hers and she sank her teeth deep into his shoulder, which only had him coming all over again. It was the most intense orgasm of his entire life. When he came back to his senses he realized that he had gotten caught up in the moment and bitten her as well. Her blood was the sweetest ambrosia in his mouth as he swallowed it down. Then he carefully pulled his teeth back and sealed the wounds with his tongue.

She seemed to be doing the same thing to her own set of marks on his neck and the feel of her little tongue licking over his skin had his spent cock reviving inside of her.

"I'm sorry I bit you. I didn't mean to," he said, slowly pulling out of her warmth, knowing she must be tender.

The satiated look on her face as he gazed down at her was making him wish that they were up in his bed instead of the study, as he would have enjoyed spending hours putting that look on her face over and over again.

"Well I certainly meant to bite you, and besides, I quite enjoyed the feel of your teeth inside of me," she said, stretching out along the table beneath him, looking very much like the contented cat she was.

That was an odd comment. He knew that a vampire's bite was pleasurable during sex, but something nagged at the back of his brain about why she'd mean to bite him as well. Unfortunately, most of his blood was still in areas *other* than his brain.

Just as he stood up and reached for his pants the study doors opened and Molly came whistling in with a tray of cookies and drinks in her hands. All three of them stopped in their tracks as Molly took in the scene before her. When her eyes locked on Viktor's neck and lit up, he didn't know what to think.

"Oh! Beggin' your pardon, sir!" Molly said as she

set the tray down on the nearest table. "So you've mated him, then? How lovely! You'll be staying with us, Miss Halle?"

"You bet, Molly," Halle said, as she climbed off the table and picked up the discarded shirt of Viktor's that she had been wearing and slipped it on. Those words sank in, and just like that, he remembered why he'd never slept with a shifter before.

"What the hell!" he said, turning to look at her. "Did you just mate mark me?"

Chapter Fifteen

"I sure did," Halle said with a smile, feeling pretty pleased with herself as she finished buttoning what was left of the closures on his shirt over her tender breasts. "Oh, are these oatmeal, Molly?"

Viktor was still standing there shocked as Halle dove on the warm cookies and milk. Molly sighed as if she'd just heard the sweetest love story ever and then retreated back to her kitchen.

"Why would you do this, Halle? Do you have any idea how much danger this puts you in?" he said furiously as he did up his pants.

Halle tried to compose herself enough to hide the sliver of hurt that snuck into her heart at his reaction to the news that they were now mated. As a shifter, she knew that even though he was a different species, he would have felt the pull of the mating heat, but she also had to expect that due to the fact that she hadn't given him a fair warning he would fight it at least a little. After all, she was probably not exactly the type of woman he usually got involved with. But she would just have to show him that she could make him happy.

"I did what fate dictated, Viktor. You are my mate, and I am yours," she told him softly as she put the cookie down, put her hands on his hips and looked up at him. "I know you feel drawn to me as much as I am to you. This is meant to be. Now Conrad has no claim over me, and we can spend our lives together."

She could see the wheels turning in his head, but she also saw the worry flare in his eyes when she'd said Conrad's name. Viktor had known him a lot longer than she had, and his expression had her worried that the douchebag vamp might not give up on owning her as easily as she thought.

Well, both of these vampires would find out right now that she wasn't the meek little kitten they thought she was. She was a predator in her own right, and she would fight to protect what was hers.

First things first, though, she needed to call her family and let them know that she was now mated. She cringed at the thought that they must have been informed by Conrad that his nemesis had abducted her, but Dori had been insistent that she didn't call them. Jeepers, they must be thinking the worst of Viktor by now.

But Viktor had also assured her that it was safer to not contact her family right away. If Conrad had gone back to her parents and found out that she had conspired to evade the blood debt purposely, things could end very badly for her father. So it was better that they had not known anything about the situation when she'd first taken off with Viktor.

The two of them also had to register their mating with the Para Council, which would at least keep them safe from Conrad trying to steal her back to force breed her. Well, legally anyway. But she knew just as well as anyone that the coven leader was *not* the rule abiding citizen he pretended to be. She didn't want to pull her family into a war, but now if Conrad tried to take her from her mate, then by shifter standards she would be well within her rights to kill in self-defense.

****

Viktor knew his reaction to the fact that she'd just mated him had hurt her feelings, and immediately he felt the need to fix it. But in all the possible outcomes of their having sex, her up and marking him as her mate had never even been one that had crossed his mind. How was it possible that the Universe would be so cruel as to saddle a sweet, beautiful creature like Halle with a baggage-heaped mess like him?

She was so incredibly beautiful, looking up at him with those luminous green eyes. It had been so long since Viktor had felt this alive. So long since he had felt like he had been living at all, really. But he knew Conrad, and if that bastard had wanted Halle before, then the news that his greatest enemy had mated her would only mean that she was in greater danger now than ever.

How in the hell am I going to keep her safe?

The only logical answer was to eliminate Conrad once and for all, and then he would be free to do what he'd been too frightened to do for centuries. He would start his life over.

He leaned down and kissed her, and then he pulled her in close for a hug.

"Okay, love. We need to figure this out because as much as you'd like to hope, Conrad isn't just going to go away," he said looking down at her again.

Her beaming smile at his acceptance of their union made his heart trip in his chest. For a vampire as old as he was, who'd thought his heart died long ago, that reaction alone was enough to make him believe in this mating.

"I need to call my parents, and we need to register our mating. At least that way if anything happens, we will be justified in protecting ourselves," she said, hugging him back.

"You can use the phone in my office to call your parents. I'd take you to them tonight, but I'm afraid Conrad will probably still be having them watched for any sign of you and it wouldn't be safe. He can't find you here. I've paid a fortune for the wards that keep my home hidden," he said as he led her to the small office connecting to the study. "I'll give you some privacy to make your call."

Viktor left the office, needing to make his own

call. He wanted to make sure that he could trust whoever would be registering their mating within the Para Council. The last thing they needed was some random clerk getting paid off by Conrad to "accidentally" shelve their paperwork and leave that bastard an opportunity to legally get Halle back into his custody. He walked over to his favorite chair in the study and the bookshelf directly behind it. There he pulled out an expensive black ledger book and sat down with his cell phone in hand. In the years since he'd been reborn into a world of blood and monsters, there had been plenty of opportunities to lend his skills as a warrior—for a price, of course.

After the first couple of centuries in his new vampire life, he had amassed enough wealth to sustain him indefinitely, so his payment requirements to lend his formidable warrior skills had turned into favors owed. Of which he kept meticulous records. Back in the day, when he was still angry and bitter at what his life had become, he'd used to relish using these favors owed to their full extent.

Taking what his new allies treasured most, watching them crumble at the thought of giving up their most prized possessions. But eventually, even his rage grew weary of the games. Suddenly he found himself offering his assistance to those in dire circumstances not because he wanted a favor owed, but because he found that the buried parts of the man he used to be simply could not stand back and watch terrible things happen to those who did not deserve it.

Of course, for reputation's sake, he would still set the price of his help, but it was a rare thing these days for him to ever cash in these favors. As he looked through the ledger to find the name he was looking for, he thought back to the night when he had collected the debt.

Viktor had been out one night and found a young

council Hunter, just barely out of training, surrounded and about to be dinner for a group of rogue vampires. The bargain was struck, and he'd saved him. Now all his years of waiting had paid off because that young Hunter had matured and advanced in his role with the Para Council. This man was now exactly the person who could ensure that their mating paperwork was filed and acknowledged as quickly as possible. He dialed the number written next to the name and waited for the man to answer.

"This is Maleck," was all the bear on the other end of the phone said in a rumbling, deep drawl.

"Burton Maleck, this is Viktor Krescech, and I am calling in your blood debt owed to me."

"Fuck," Burton muttered. "I was wondering when the devil would come for his due. What do you want? If this has anything to do with you kidnapping the Briggs girl, then I can't help you. Conrad has already reported you to the council."

"I assumed as much, and this *is* about Halle Briggs. We need to register our mating with the Para Council, and I need *you* to make sure that Conrad won't bury it and attempt to reclaim her by force," Viktor answered, trying to remain calm.

He'd suspected that Conrad would report him to the Para Council eventually, but given the way that the bastard had manipulated Halle's family into the blood debt in the first place, Viktor had thought he'd drag his feet on it.

There were a few moments of silence on the other end of the phone. Of course, the shifter was probably trying to figure out which one of the reputed homicidal vampires was lying to him.

"You're serious," Burton said carefully. "Halle has mated you, and it was consensual?"

The abrupt laugh that came out of Viktor when he replayed the circumstance of their mating in his head was as much a surprise to himself as it must have been to the man on the other end of the phone.

"Well, she didn't exactly *ask* me before she decided to do it. On the other hand, I wasn't complaining at the time," he answered honestly. "But I feel the bond as strongly as she does."

It must have been the correct answer because he could hear the tone in Burton's voice relax as he laughed as well.

"Yeah well, I have news for you. With shifter females, that's just the beginning of their bossy tendencies," Burton said before he paused once more. "You know, Krescech, when you saved my life all those years ago, I truly couldn't reconcile the man who I'd met with the monster that everyone proclaims you to be. But I'm damned well relieved that a sweet girl like Halle is going to end up with you instead of that bastard, Conrad Dair. I'll have your paperwork drawn up, but you know that the rest of the council is going to need to see Halle to confirm that you're mated. You'll have to bring her in."

"I know," Viktor said, trying not to think about how dangerous it would be for them to go to the Para Council building where Conrad no doubt had dozens of spies waiting for them to turn up. "Conrad will be trying to stop us. Can you gather the Council and not tell them who the mating confirmation is for? I don't trust anyone but you not to leak this to him."

"I'll come up with something. Just make sure you have her here at nine tomorrow morning," Burton said before he hung up.

Now all they had to do was walk past a network of supernatural spies and evade a psychotic megalomaniac who was trying to steal and force mate his new bride. How hard could that be?

Viktor was certain they were going to find out.

Chapter Sixteen

Halle walked out of the office as Viktor was ending his own call. She'd overheard a little bit of the end of his conversation and didn't know how concerned she should be. The phone call to her family had gone about as well as she'd expected. They were relieved that she was okay but were kind of freaking out about the whole "mated to a well-known killer" scenario.

All she could do was plead with them to trust her cat's instincts and be supportive. So she hoped that her father didn't send out a lynch mob to relieve her of her new husband or anything. Especially since she'd finally found out what the big deal was about all this sex business—and she had grown rather fond of him so far. He turned towards her, and once again she found herself admiring how handsome he was. After the pleasure that Viktor had given her, she was having a hard time focusing on anything but getting his clothes off again.

"Everything okay with your family, love?" he asked, as he put his phone away and pulled her into a hug.

She loved that Viktor was affectionate without even thinking. Her cat purred as she nuzzled into her mate's strong chest. Halle didn't want Viktor to get off on the wrong foot with her family, so she thought she'd omit their concerns for the time being. She knew they were just being protective and was confident that when they finally got to spend some time with him, they would realize he was a good man. She just smiled and nodded back in answer. Her tummy picked that moment to start to rumble, much to her eternal embarrassment.

"Sounds like you're hungry. Shall we go and find Molly to see if dinner is ready? The smell of that prime rib has been making my mouth water all afternoon," he said, as he leaned down to give her a quick kiss, then took her hand to lead her down the hall.

When they entered the kitchen, conversation abruptly stopped between the two brownies standing over by the sink. From how close they were standing, Halle could only assume that the older male who'd interrupted them in the library was Molly's husband, whom the friendly brownie had been telling her all about since she'd arrived. His eyes took a look down at Viktor's hand holding Halle's tight, and a huge smile broke out on the slight male's face.

"So it's true, then?" Gerald asked excitedly. "Molly wasna' jesting, you really have taken this little beauty as a mate?"

"Yes, Gerald, it is true." Viktor sighed dramatically. "This is Halle. Halle, this is Gerald. He runs my household, and is Molly's husband."

"I'm so glad to meet you, Halle. We've been hoping that Master Viktor would find a nice girl like you and settle down," the sweet little man said, as he took her hand in greeting.

Halle heard Viktor sigh beside her again and almost felt his exaggerated eye roll, but she could also tell how much these two meant to him from the change in his tone of voice when he spoke to them.

"Before you two start to do a happy dance now that you've finally seen me married off, can we please get some dinner? Halle is hungry."

At those words, Molly *did* do a happy little hop and started to bustle around the kitchen almost faster than they could see.

Brownies. They were a little on the creepy side if you watched them work, like little Tasmanian devils, zipping around at five times the normal speed. Halle hadn't really been up close to any before, as her father employed mostly members of their pard in his household and businesses, so she was mesmerized.

"Would you like to take supper in the dining room, sir?" Gerald asked, seeming to have recovered from the shock of Viktor's announcement.

Halle did the calculations in her head, and while she *was* super hungry, her cat was also clawing at her to satisfy a different kind of appetite. She had twenty-three years of abstinence and sexual frustration to make up for, after all. If they ate in the dining room, it would take even longer before they could find some privacy and she could explore her new mate properly, and that just wouldn't do.

"Actually, Gerald," she asked in a sweet voice, "would it be possible for us to have dinner in Viktor's suite? You know, so we can enjoy some *private time*?"

She felt Viktor's hand tighten on hers, and when he looked over at her she knew by the heat in his eyes that he'd understood the implications of her request perfectly.

"Of course, Mistress Halle, you two go on upstairs. I'll bring supper up in few moments for you," the brownie answered with a wink.

Before she could thank Gerald, Viktor had scooped her up off her feet and raced to his suite at vampire speed, so fast she practically had whiplash.

"I guess you're hungry, too, huh?" she teased, as he set her on her feet and then instantly reached for the buttons that were barely holding her shirt together.

"Indeed I am, love, but you have far too many clothes on at the moment to satisfy my appetite," he said, as he continued to unbutton his way down her shirt.

But Halle had formulated a plan when she'd suggested this. Downstairs, her mating heat had been so overwhelming in the study that she could barely even remember what Viktor had looked like naked, other than super-hot, of course. But now that she finally had time, and a male of her very own, she wanted to explore every inch of him at her leisure. This also meant that she couldn't let him distract her with his seductive ways.

"Hold on, mate," she said, gently batting his huge hands away.

She almost had to laugh at the confused expression on his face when he looked up at her. It was as if someone had taken his favorite toy away and not given a reason why.

"It's my turn to explore *you*. I want to kiss every inch of your delectable body," she purred in her sexiest voice, as she turned them around and pushed him back to lie on the huge bed in his room. "So it's *your* turn to get naked."

"I supposed I wouldn't be a very supportive mate if I argued with that, now would I?" he answered with a sexy smile as he turned those nimble fingers back on his own shirt buttons.

When his shirt finally dropped to the ground and he fell back against the bed, Halle's heart fluttered in her chest just to look at Viktor lying there. His skin was like marble perfection, so smooth and pale, each muscle carefully chiseled out as if by a master artist. Halle had seen her fair share of naked men throughout her life. Shifters did, after all, grow up being used to nudity. It was just a natural part of shifting, and even though she'd snuck more than a peek at the handsome males in her pard during group shifts, her over-protective father and brother had made certain that she'd never had the opportunity to touch, and her fingers were itching to run all over her new mate.

Chapter Seventeen

Viktor wasn't sure if he could endure all that Halle had planned for him, but he was willing to do his best to try for her. The first few passes of her delicate hands over his bare chest were hesitant, but as she started to grow bolder in her exploration, he could feel the sweat begin to bead on his forehead as the desire built up inside of him. Once her tiny hands made their way to the button at the waist of his pants, he was almost growling.

She looked up at his face, a small smile blooming before she let go of the button and moved her hand lower to caress his swollen cock through the material of his trousers.

"I like it when you growl at me, Viktor. It makes me want to do naughty things to you," she said, as she continued to tease him with her hands.

Her statement only had him growling louder at her. He wanted her soft little hands stroking his aching flesh already. When she finally undid the button and released the zipper, she gasped when his shaft sprang forward into her waiting hands. Viktor quickly raised his hips and got rid of his pants as she stared mesmerized at his cock. The longer she stared, the harder it got, and when a bead of pre-cum emerged on the tip she absently licked her lips, making him groan out loud.

"Gods, Halle, I want your mouth on me so badly," he said, as he took her hand in his and gently wrapped it around his aching shaft.

"You're so soft and hard at the same time," she said, as she took a few tentative strokes up and down. "I wasn't expecting that."

When she leaned in and her hot breath tickled across his skin, his heart almost stopped, but when her little pink tongue flicked out and collected the moisture on the tip of his cock, he was almost certain he was going to be the first vampire in history to expire from cardiac arrest.

"I love the taste of you, Viktor," she purred, her eyes meeting his. "I want more."

"Yes, suck me, baby." Viktor's answer was barely recognizable with how deep his voice had gone with desire.

When his new little mate wrapped her luscious lips around his cock and took him all the way to the root, he had to grip the headboard to keep his fingers from curling in her hair to direct her movements. Viktor tried to remember that this was her first time doing this and he didn't want to scare her away. Sweet Goddess, with how incredible this felt, he wanted her to do it as much and as often as possible.

It had been so long since Viktor had engaged in sex with a woman he actually cared about, the emotional side of it was almost overwhelming him. When she urged his legs farther apart and her mouth began kissing and licking its way down his shaft until she reached his balls below, he tried to recount his favorite ledger entries to keep his mind off coming like a randy teenager. He was doing quite well until she made her way back up his dick with her talented tongue and began to massage his balls with her hand. Then after she took him fully back into the hot recesses of her mouth and began to suckle at him, she added some strange twirl with her other hand and, just like that, he lost all control over his body.

"Ah, I'm going to come if you don't stop, baby," Viktor growled out, as his hips began to pump into her mouth and hands.

Halle looked up at him, her eyes full of raging desire, and he'd never seen anything more beautiful in all his life.

"I want to see you come," she said as she lifted her mouth from his flesh. "Will you do that for me?"

"Of course," he said softly, her request reminding him to be gentle with her. "Here, climb up and straddle my thighs."

Halle looked curious as to what Viktor intended, and when she swung her leg over to straddle his legs, he growled again when he saw how drenched she was.

"Did you like that, baby?" Viktor growled low, the smell of her desire causing his teeth to extend. "Did you like licking and sucking on my hard cock?"

Viktor could see her panting increase at his dirty words, and he was glad she responded so freely. It would be such a pleasure to explore his new little mate's sexuality. He would enjoy every second of showing her a whole new world.

"Yes, I loved it," she whispered, as she settled her ass over his upper thighs.

He met her eyes and kept the contact as he brought his hands up to cup her ass, and then he slowly moved her up so that her wet folds were nestled right up against his achingly hard cock. He loved the sound of her gasp as he took his shaft and rubbed it back and forth against her swollen clit. He knew it wouldn't take much for him to come all over her stomach at this point so he moved one of her hands to cover his and guided her until she took over.

"Watch us together love. I want you to use me to rub that little clit until you're coming all over my cock, and then I'll come just for you." Viktor panted, trying like hell to wait until she came first, but her pussy felt like hot silk over his skin.

Her eyes flashed to feline as her lust increased even further and he could see her fangs clearly now as she bit her lower lip. Viktor had lived for a very long time, but he'd never seen anything sexier than his mate above him right now, her hand moving furiously to chase after her orgasm. He almost thought he had lost the battle holding his own back until her hips started to buck and she finally moaned his name out loud while still gripping his cock firmly. Her eyes closed as she sighed in pleasure, and that was the sound that broke the rest of his self-control.

"Baby, watch me." He urged her to open her eyes because he couldn't wait any longer.

As she watched, his cock erupted, releasing all over her stomach as she leaned back to rest on his thighs. The look on her face was full of possession and wonder, and it left him getting hard all over again even before the last of his orgasm cooled on her skin.

He pulled her forward for a long, slow kiss, and settled her on his chest.

"Wow," she whispered, as she ran her hands up and down his body. "That was extremely hot."

"I agree. Where on earth did you learn that trick with twisting your hand if you'd never done that before?" he asked, gathering her up and carrying her into the en suite bathroom.

"Oh," she said with an adorable blush. "I like to read."

"Well, you will have the largest library possible then, as the results were undeniable," he answered with a wink before he turned on the shower and stepped into the steam with her still cuddled in his arms.

That had her laughing, and it was the sweetest sound he'd ever heard. He slowly lowered her to her feet and began to gently soap her soft skin up when her stomach growled loudly and her face turned a charming shade of pink.

"I guess we forgot to eat again," she said, as she

washed him as well. "I'm still surprised you eat at all really. I didn't know that vampires ate food. It's been driving me crazy all week not asking about it, but I didn't know if you'd consider that rude or not. I haven't spent much time around vampires before."

"You can ask me anything you'd like, Halle. I like that you're curious about me. It's different for every vampire. We can eat food, and if we do it reduces our need for blood. But many of the older ones were made in a time when it was easier to find a blood donor than a good meal, so it's habit for them, I suppose," he answered absently, as he rinsed them both and turned off the water. "Gerald left our dinner in the hall while we were—occupied. We can eat it in bed, and then it's my turn to devour *you,* kitten."

Chapter Eighteen

Halle was starting to get a little nervous as she stepped into the large shower all alone the next morning. The night before, after a lovely dinner of delicious prime rib that they'd eaten snuggled up in bed, Viktor had spent hours making love to her until they'd finally drifted off to sleep exhausted. This morning, however, the Viktor she'd woken up next to was not the same man who'd held her all night. He was back to the distant warrior she'd first met, and it was freaking her out. She knew that he was worried about going in to see the Para Council today and for a male so capable to worry about it? Well, that, in turn, worried her even more, so when Dori magically popped into the bathroom as she was stepping out of the shower, Halle was relieved to see the fairy.

"Dori! I'm kind of freaking out here. How is this going to go today?" she asked, as she dried herself off. "Conrad is going to be there, isn't he?"

Dori certainly wasn't looking like her sassy, sarcastic self when Halle asked after Conrad, which only made the butterflies in her stomach ten times worse.

"As your Fairy Godmother, I am only allowed to show you the path to your Happy Ever After. The rest is supposed to be up to you. But I do have a message I *can* give you, Halle: don't be afraid to fight for what is yours. You're stronger than you think," Dori said with a wink and stole a quick hug before she disappeared.

"Dori! Get back here. What the hell is that supposed to mean?" Halle yelled at the mirror.

The bathroom door burst open and Viktor rushed in ready for battle.

"Are you all right, Halle?" he growled, looking frantically around. "Who were you yelling at?"

"What? Oh, it was just a little pep talk to my reflection before we go," she answered with a fake smile, hoping that her face wasn't flaming red with embarrassment for being caught supposedly yelling at herself. "I'm almost ready."

She saw him visibly relax when he confirmed that she was alone in the bathroom.

"Molly brought you some new clothes, love. I laid them out on the bed for you," he said as he walked up and kissed her. "We need to go in forty minutes. I intend to leave as little a time gap as possible between our arrival and our appointment time for things to go wrong."

"Okay, no problem," she answered, trying to sound a lot braver than she was feeling.

"Molly has breakfast ready for us downstairs," Viktor said before he took her hand. "I know you're worried, Halle, but it will be okay. In a few hours, we'll be back here and we can start planning our life together."

"I know, I've just never had this much to lose before, and it's scaring the hell out of me." She stepped into his arms and snuggled close.

"I have no intention of losing you, now that I've found you, Halle. The universe couldn't be so cruel."

Halle just stood there in his arms, soaking up the warmth. She hoped that the universe wasn't going to screw them over this morning. She hoped that she'd done enough to ensure Conrad wouldn't get his way. But then again, she knew from experience that the world wasn't a fair place.

She could barely eat as they sat at the table downstairs. She knew that Viktor had to be just as worried as she was when she saw Molly and Gerald join them for breakfast. In the week that she'd been there, not once had the other couple sat and eaten with them. When breakfast was over, Molly gathered her into a tight hug.

"I wish that we could go with you, love, but here, let me send a little bit of me own protection with ya," the small woman said, as she placed an old amulet around Halle's neck. Halle could feel the wild magic in it, and it sent a shiver through her.

Brownies were technically categorized as under-fae and had a magic that was much different from that of shifters and vampires. It was raw and wild, and they could manipulate it in many different ways. You never wanted to offend any of the under-fae species as they could become quite unpredictable and aggressive. But they were also fiercely protective once they'd taken a liking to you, and Halle felt blessed to have won over the sweet female.

"You both take care now. We'll be making you a grand dinner tonight to celebrate your official mating. We *will* be seeing you soon," Gerald added with a confident nod, as he put his arm around his wife's small shoulders.

"Thank you, Gerald. That makes me feel better," Viktor said, as he took Halle's hand and led her out to the car.

"What was that all about?" Halle asked as they pulled out of the drive.

"Gerald's great-grandmother was a full fae noblewoman. He has the gift of foresight passed down from her. He doesn't see things all the time, but he has saved my ass on more than one occasion over the years. Although, brownies are a tricky lot, so hopefully that wasn't just him trying to make us feel better about us driving off to our impending doom," he said with a small smile.

"They've been with you a long time, haven't they?"

"Over sixty years now. Molly's family has worked for me for three generations, and brownies can live to be hundreds of years old. They're the closest thing to family I've had since I was turned."

"Well I hope they're right about dinner then," Halle said, as she took his hand in hers and wrapped the other around the necklace Molly had given her.

Chapter Nineteen

They were about two blocks from the Council Building, waiting for a red light to change when suddenly Halle's hackles rose. She had two seconds to look towards Viktor before the driver's door was ripped right off its hinges, and two huge grey, unnatural arms reached inside and grabbed her mate, dragging him away.

"Halle!"

"Viktor!" she screamed his name at the same time he did hers. She reached for him, but the door on her side opened up as well and she glanced at the smirking vamp as her fangs slid down with a growl.

"Now, now, pretty kitty." The stranger pointed a gun at her as he slowly took a step back. "Conrad doesn't want you hurt, but I'll shoot you if you come at me."

"What do you want? Where is Viktor?" She glanced around her, but couldn't see her mate or the grey monster that had pulled him out of the car.

"Viktor is busy right now, trying not to lose his head to an ogre, I imagine."

"I'll kill you." Her heart almost stopped when she thought about something happening to Viktor. "I swear I will."

"Making sure that no one gets killed to today is up to you. You've got that part right, Halle." His face was no longer smiling. "We have more than just Viktor, as I have no doubt that eventually, he'll get away from that beast—he always does. But I'm afraid Tavin won't be so lucky. Conrad has your brother, and if you don't come with me and do what he says, your brother will lose his life today."

She couldn't breathe. This couldn't be true. She was so fucking close to being happy—why couldn't fate just leave them be?

"Why should I just believe that you have my brother?"

The vamp dialed his phone and held it up for her as it rang until finally it connected and Conrad's cruel face filled the screen.

"Do you have her, Joe? Ah, sweet Halle, so good to see your beautiful face once again." The asshole had the nerve to smile at her, like they were old friends. "Such an angry look, however, I'm assuming that means you didn't offer to come willingly? Here … let your brother convince you otherwise."

He stepped back, and she cried out to see her strong, big brother, strapped to a chair and bleeding from too many places to count. One of the skanky vampire bitches was leisurely lapping at the blood dripping from a cut right below his collarbone.

"Don't go with him, Halle! Stay away from this bastard! Find Krescech!"

But her brother's words were cut off by his own scream as the woman sank her teeth deep into his neck.

"Stop!" she screamed. "Stop it! What do you want?"

"Just what was promised to me is all, my dear," Conrad answered calmly. "Let Joe bring you to me and you fulfill your mating agreement with me in front of the Council, and your darling brother will be sent back to your pard safe and sound. You have my word on that."

"The word of a sociopath? Even if I agreed, Conrad, it's too late," she sobbed. "I found my true mate, and we've marked each other. I am already mated."

She waited for the other shoe to drop, for the horrible consequences of her telling Conrad the truth, but he just laughed instead.

"Silly girl, you think I care if you are already

mated?" he sneered. "Your genes will ensure me an heir regardless of if you are my mate or not, which is all that I require from you. Taking you away from that irritating bastard Krescech is simply a lovely bonus to make my day even brighter than it already is."

Halle's heart raced as she hoped against hope that Viktor would suddenly appear and save her. Her mind tried to come up with a plan, but there was nothing she could think of besides going along with this monster to save her brother.

"Don't think too long, dear—your brother doesn't have that much blood left in him to give…"

"Fine!" She broke when Tavin's groan sounded out from behind Conrad. "I'll go with him and do what you want. But you'd better keep your bargain, Dair, or so help me, I will find a way to end you."

"As soon as our mating paperwork is signed, your brother will be released."

Halle took one more look around them, hoping to catch a glimpse of Viktor before she slid into the car with Joe. She said a prayer to the Goddess that he was all right. She didn't know anything about ogres, but anything that could have surprised her mate and taken off with him like that had to be a frightening opponent. Silent tears ran down her cheeks. It had only taken minutes for her entire world to implode, her dreams of happiness plowed over by some megalomaniac's master plan. She knew for a certainty that she would never allow Conrad to bring a child of hers into his sick care. Once Tavin was safe back with the pard, Halle would do whatever it took to make sure that never happened. She was the only female in the family line of childbearing age, so his plan would end with her, freeing the rest of her family from his debt. If death was the only way to flee him, then she would have to be brave enough.

VIKTOR

****

"I will kill you for this, beast!" Viktor raged as he tried to break free of the ogre's hold. The male had grabbed him and the next thing he knew, they were suddenly running through the woods. Viktor had desperately tried to subdue him and get back to his mate, but the thing's arms were like an ungiving vise that he could not escape.

"I have no quarrel with you, vampire," the deep, echoing voice answered back.

"No quarrel?" Viktor's voice was high in disbelief. "You just took me away so I cannot protect my mate from a madman who wishes to mate and enslave her against her will!"

"I simply collected what I was told, I have not harmed you," he answered almost nonchalantly. "I made a bargain with Dair to get my cousin out of his debt. I am to hold you for thirty minutes, no less, no more."

"Where are we? How did we get here?"

"We traced, of course," The beast looked at him like Viktor was slow, but he'd never heard of an ogre having the ability to trace before. There was more to this one than brute strength, so he needed to be cautious.

"I didn't realize that ogres could travel that way."

"They can't." The large, dark eyes stared back at him, unblinking.

"But, you just *did*," Viktor screamed in frustration. This creature had to be being deliberately obtuse, and he didn't have time for such games. He needed to get back to his mate.

Viktor didn't want to think about what Halle must be going through right now. She must be terrified. He tried to break free of the beast once again, thrashing and biting at every exposed inch of skin.

"You are quite persistent—and wiggly, but you

cannot harm me. You will only harm yourself if you insist on this." The coal black eyes peered down at him. "Dair said he would not harm the girl, that she was contracted to him through her family. He said that you had stolen her and held her against her will."

"Conrad is a lying bastard! Halle and I are true mates, and we were on our way to the council to register our mating officially. All he wants is an heir from her, and he would take what she is unwilling to give."

It was odd to watch the words he'd just spoken seem to sink into the mind of the huge grey beast, and when his overly large brow began to furrow in anger, hope began to blossom in Viktor's chest.

"He would force her?" The deep voice was surprisingly gentle. "I don't abide by that at all."

"Will you help me get her back then? Do you know where he's taken her? I can pay you anything you want."

Viktor wasn't one to normally ask for help from others, but things were different now. He had Halle to protect and he would do anything to make that happen.

"I try not to get involved in things in the outside world," the large beast sighed.

"Well, then you should have left me alone to protect my mate."

"…and that is exactly why I try to keep to myself. Why don't people just leave me alone?" His big stone, grey shoulders slumped in defeat, and Viktor almost yelped as he was released and he fell to the ground, "I will show you where Conrad is, and then I'm going home—where other people aren't."

With those final words, the huge ogre put his meaty paw on Viktor's shoulder and then suddenly, everything went black.

Chapter Twenty

"What the hell is going on, Dori? Halle's been taken by that awful man!" her mother screeched behind her, scaring the bejesus right out of her.

"Son of bitch, Mom! Don't sneak up on me like that or I'm gonna make you wear a bell!"

"Aren't you going to do something to rescue her?"

Her mother's hands were now flailing all over the damned place, and of course, she could see how there might be some concern for the little leopard's welfare—if you didn't have the inside track like Dori did. She'd put all the players in motion after all. Conrad would have never been able to get Barrett out of his ogre hidey-hole if not for her, and without this little deviation from the plan, there would have been no Happy Ending for Halle's adorable big brother, Tavin. Which of course she couldn't have. Super-hot leopard shifters did not get sucked dry and ganked by a group of douchey vamps on Dori's watch, no siree.

"Relax, Mom, you've got to have a little more faith than that." She began the countdown to when the cavalry would arrive, "…and three, two, one. Bam! View crystal switch to channel two, Viktor."

When the swirling mist cleared from the crystal, it showed a well-manicured back yard in what appeared to be any random neighborhood, but then suddenly, two beings were there, standing beside the shrubbery, one very large, grey mass of muscles and one very angry, handsome vampire.

"Hey, isn't that your mechanic?" Her mom's face scrunched up and took a closer look before Dori tried to shove her away.

"What? Nah, that's just some rando ogre, never

seen him before." She avoided her mom's lie detecting eye-contact. "Now shh, this is where it all comes together."

"Oh!" Her mom's excited whisper was almost right next to her ear, crowding her. "Is this where Viktor rescues Halle again from the bad guys?"

"Nah, Conrad left about seven minutes ago with her, they're en route to the Council Building to get the mating papers signed."

"What!"

Her dear old mom's shrill scream totally scattered the crystal's magic, and it went dark right before Viktor was about to break down the back door to the house.

"Thanks a lot, Ma." She sighed and threw her hands up. "Now I'm going to have to do it old school and go monitor this in person!"

Dori sighed loudly and turned to attempt to stuff her laptop back into her bag without crushing all her other super important stuff, like the Cheetos and chocolate almond Pocky sticks.

"This is precisely the kind of hitch that sends all those inferior Fairy Godmother's crying into their cotton candy milkshakes. I've planned everything right down to the minutiae. Just because I didn't give my clients the heads up on how things were going to unfold, doesn't mean I'm not prepared for it," she muttered as she turned back to give the crystal ball a flick with her fingers to see if she could get the signal back.

"But why couldn't you tell them? Halle must be freaking out!" Her mom's voice surprised her.

"Oh, you're still here. I thought I was just talking to myself."

Her mom's eyes narrowed and then her arms came up to cross over her chest, and Dori knew she'd screwed up.

"I'm sorry!" she yelped.

"Too late, I'm emailing your therapist for her to put this on your 'we're working on it' list." Her mother's smug smile had Dori groaning in anticipated emotional pain.

"Ah, Mom, that means she's going to make me go out and 'interact' with other people in public so that I learn to pay attention when other people are in the room." She purposely air-quoted the word interact, as she was anticipating utter failure. "She'll probably make us go to the Stop 'N' Shop and say yes to all those little old ladies trying to peddle their free samples. Who wants free samples of yogurt? No one! That's who! You know I don't trust strangers … or grocery stores. You always end up buying more than you actually need, and how are you supposed to trust that you really wanted to try the spicy Kraft Dinner, or if you only got sucked into buying it because it had a cool display beside the Doritos? They are manipulating us at every turn, I tell you!"

Chapter Twenty-One

"Okay I'm here, now let my brother go just like you agreed." Halle stood her ground in front of Conrad, even though being this close to him made her skin crawl.

"Not that I don't trust you, my dear," he stepped closer and walked a slow circle around her, "but I will release your brother as soon as your signature is next to mine on those mating papers. I wouldn't want to think you had some foolish hope of double-crossing me."

"Of course not."

There goes that plan.

"I'm insulted that you would even think that." She lifted her chin to look down on him. Okay, even Halle had to admit that it was a weak protest, but come on! *Of course,* she was going to try to save her brother and then bail on this creep. Who wouldn't?

"Well then, my little bride," Conrad held out his arm for her to take and she forced herself to accept. "Shall we make our way to the Council Building?"

Halle took a deep breath and tried to keep calm. What was that Dori had told her right before they'd left this morning? *I am stronger than I know.* All she could do was pray that her Fairy Godmother was right because she needed to figure out a plan before they signed those papers, and leaving her brother to die at the hands of hungry vamps wasn't going to happen.

****

"Halle!" Viktor yelled as he kicked in the back door of the little suburban home the ogre had traced them to. A thousand scenarios of what she could be enduring right now swam through his head, making him crazed. He knew he wasn't being careful, but damned if he could help himself.

"By all means," the ogre muttered as he followed

Viktor inside, "let us *not* use the element of surprise when attacking a house that is possibly full of hungry vampires."

Viktor grabbed the first vamp that came running into the kitchen by the throat, holding him up against the wall. "Where is she?"

His only answer was hissing and flailing arms as he slowly cut off the man's air supply, hoping to entice him to answer. Two more vamps came swarming in and were literally batted away by the ogre's giant grey arms. Over and over again, he would punt them into the next room and they would come back trying to get to Viktor and their ally.

"Tell me or die," he demanded, and the bastard finally broke just as his pale skin began to turn a disturbing shade of puce.

"Conrad took her," the garbled words sputtered out. "He took her to the council building to sign the papers…"

"You lie!" Viktor spat back at him. "Halle is my mate, and she would never sign those papers!"

"Hmm, I think I know how Conrad convinced her…" The ogre's booming voice came from the next room, getting Viktor's attention. He hadn't noticed that the beast must have gotten bored playing with the other vamps, who now lay unconscious on the kitchen floor.

Viktor slammed the man's head into the wall hard enough to have his eyes rolling back and closing, and he dropped him to the floor before following the deep voice, which was now talking to someone. He came to an abrupt stop when he rounded the corner and saw a man tied to a chair in the middle of the empty living room. He was covered in blood and bite marks, but his scent marked him as a leopard shifter. His blond hair and familiar facial features clued Viktor in that this man was most likely the brother of his mate—and the reason that she would have willingly left him behind to go with Conrad.

He felt like such a failure. The fates had been so generous as to bless him with the gift of a mate such as Halle, and he couldn't even protect her. She'd sacrificed herself to save her brother, so she must have thought she had no other choice. How could she know that Viktor would bring down hell itself to get to her?

"Leave me! You have to go after Halle!" the leopard moaned as soon as the ogre removed the gag.

"We shouldn't leave you. You need medical care—plus the vamps aren't dead, and they will be hungry once they wake…" The huge grey head cocked to the side and looked back at Viktor in question. "Should I kill them so we can leave this one here?"

"Who *are* you?" the shifter asked.

"I'm Viktor, your sister's mate," he answered. "This is Barrett the ogre, and he allowed Conrad's men to take your sister from me."

"Hey—I *told* you what the arrangement was. Now you're just trying to make me feel bad." The huge male frowned as he reached forward to snap the ties holding the shifter's hands and feet to the chair.

"Conrad grabbed me two days ago as I was leaving work. He's forcing Halle to sign the mating paperwork or he threatened to kill me. You have to go and rescue her!"

"It's Tavin, right?" Viktor asked as they helped the injured man to shaky feet. "We're all going to the Council Building to stop Conrad, so that way Halle will know you're safe. Are you strong enough for that?"

Tavin nodded.

"The Council Building? But there'll be so many *people* there." The ogre was frowning once again. "Can't

I just drop you off in front? I don't like people."

Good Goddess, this gigantic beast is ridiculous. Viktor wanted to punch him in the nose for allowing any of this to happen in the first place—but he now knew how painful and futile attempting to fist-fight with an ogre was. *I suppose an alternative motivation is the only way to go.*

"Barrett, I just need you to make sure Tavin is all right while I go after Conrad. I think you owe Halle that much for allowing them to take her in the first place, don't you?"

He almost thought his plan had backfired when the thick black eyebrows came together as the grey beast narrowed his eyes, but then the guilt slowly came through and he threw up those giant stone arms in defeat.

"Fine!" he muttered. "But you'd better make it quick and then we're even."

"Deal," Viktor quickly agreed before the ogre changed his mind. "I just have to make one call first."

Viktor tried to remain calm as the phone continued to ring in his ear, and then finally the other end picked up. "Maleck here."

"Burton, it's Viktor, we were on our way to the appointment this morning and were ambushed by Conrad's men. He has Halle and he's blackmailing her to sign the papers. I need you to stall them until I get there."

"Shit." There was the sound of frantic paper shuffling on the other end of the phone. "His name's in the fucking book for an eleven o'clock appointment. Who in the hell booked this for him?"

The bear shifter was muttering and swearing to himself on the other end of the phone. "Viktor, I'll try and stall them, but if she signs those papers in front of the council, then there isn't anything I can do. She'll belong to him."

"I know." Viktor tried to hide the fear in his voice, but he doubted he was successful by the pitied look the giant man at his side gave him. "Just do what you can, Burton. We're on our way."

They *had* to make it in time. He couldn't imagine any other outcome. If Viktor failed Halle now, he would never forgive himself.

Chapter Twenty-Two

When they pulled up in front of the Para Council building, it looked just like it had on any other day. The streets were bustling downtown and the sidewalk was filled with people all going somewhere. They were all carrying on with their lives, oblivious to the fact that *her* life and freedom were all about to end. Halle had been here several times in the past and was always amazed at how beautiful the building was. The most important people in their community made decisions here every day that affected the lives of every paranormal on this continent. But today instead of wonder, the building just felt dark and ominous. Her cat was pacing and snarling inside, wanting to lash out at the horrible man sitting beside them.

Kill him, it said. *Free us from his plans*, it pleaded. But the picture of her brother bleeding and weak was seared into her mind.

When the car came to a full stop, Conrad turned to look at her. The expression on his chiseled face was calm, and he just watched her for a moment.

"Are you ready for this, my dear?" he asked in such a reasonable tone, it just made her hate him all the more. "We have an appointment with the council, and you will be required to give your consent and sign the mating papers of your own free will. The Council members present cannot think I have coerced you in any way—do you understand, Halle? Do you understand what will happen to your brother Tavin if you fail in these tasks in the next thirty minutes?"

She felt the wave of panic rise in her chest as his words sank in. *Can I pull this off?* Inside she was screaming in rage, and her animal side was getting frantic now that it knew the cage door on their freedom was about to close. *What if I lose control of my beast and shift in front of everyone?*

"Do you need another moment?" he pushed, one eyebrow raised as if he doubted that she could do this.

Focus, Halle. She didn't need to appear happy to be doing this. It was for all intents and purposes supposed to be an arranged mating by her own family, so she just needed to hold it together enough to not look like she wanted to tear out her prospective mate's throat with her teeth. *I can do this. I* have *to do this—for Tavin's sake.*

"I'm fine, let's get this over with,"

"Indeed." Conrad opened the car door and got out.

Halle was surprised when he offered her his hand to help her, whether it was to put on a good show, or simply because he thought she might bolt—she didn't know.

She already knew that there were wards on the building that didn't allow outside weapons through the front door. So, the two thugs that were accompanying them wouldn't have their guns with them. Even the enforcers had to use alternate entry points to check their weapons in. That had been explained to them on the very first school tour of the council buildings she'd had when she was a cub. She hadn't thought much about it at the time, but now, she wondered if these rules were even able to protect people at all?

Halle felt the tension in Conrad's arm beneath hers, so he was still nervous about something, even if his face didn't betray it. The lobby wasn't very busy today. There were only about a dozen or so people milling about, probably waiting for their own appointments with the council. Conrad directed her past the general reception desk, straight on to a smaller kiosk that stood in front of the elevators that led directly to the council registration chambers.

"Conrad Dair and Halle Briggs. We have an eleven o'clock appointment with the council," Conrad said in a snooty tone, as he stared down the young wolf shifter working the desk.

"Ah, yes, Mr. Dair. I see your appointment right here," the attendant said, with a nervous voice that made the hair on the back of Halle's neck stand up in alarm. "The council seems to be running a bit behind with their previous appointment this morning. Would you like to take a seat until they're ready for you?"

"No," Conrad replied in a stone-cold voice. "Do you know who I am? You will open this elevator and let us up into the council chambers immediately, or I will separate your head from your body."

Wow, that escalated quickly, Halle thought as she watched the color abruptly drain from the attendant's face and his sheer panic set in.

"Still threatening innocent children, I see, Conrad." Halle's heart skipped a beat when the glorious sound of Viktor's voice came from behind them.

Conrad's grabbed her arm and spun them around to face Viktor, and Halle almost collapsed in relief when her cat scented her brother and she saw Tavin being held up by a giant grey man in the shadows near the front entryway. He looked horrible, but he was safe, and Viktor had come for her.

"Call security," Conrad barked to the desk attendant behind them. "This rogue vampire is trying to abduct my mate!"

When Conrad's head turned back around, however, there was a sadistic smile on his face, "Trying to take once again what doesn't belong to you, Krescech? Halle has made her choice. Are you going to slink back to the cave you've been hiding in, or am I going to have the pleasure of watching security remove you?"

"We all know you never gave Halle *or* her father a choice, but she has one now." Viktor extended his hand towards her. "Do you trust me, Halle?"

Almost all of the other people who had been minding their own business in the foyer were now watching the drama unfold. *Could it really be this easy? Can I just take Viktor's hand? Will Conrad let it happen? Surely with this many witnesses, he wouldn't cause a scene?*

Halle quickly found out as Conrad's sharp nails dug painfully into her arm when she tried to take a step towards her mate.

"I don't think so, *kitten*," he sneered in a low voice, next to her ear.

****

When Dori popped into the foyer of the Council Building, she was careful not to be seen as she stuck her head around the corner from the washrooms. This was the big showdown moment for Halle and Viktor, and they needed to prove the fates that they deserved their Happy Ever After—which meant they had to do the rest on their own, without her magical intervention. The first rule of thumb for Fairy Godmothers—even ones with her badass powers, was that you can set the fated couple on the path to their happy ending, but you can't just hand it over to them. Happiness had to be won with courage, strength of character, and more often than not, a sacrifice of some kind. Dori knew that both Halle and Viktor were worthy of their future together. They were both prepared to sacrifice all for the ones that they loved, but would Halle find the courage to *fight* for it as well?

Chapter Twenty-Three

Viktor knew it wasn't going to be that easy as soon as he saw Halle flinch in pain when she tried to walk away from Conrad. It was a delicate game they played. He didn't want to put his mate in more danger than she already was, so he couldn't attack head-on. The last thing he wanted to do was give Conrad a reason to hurt the one person who now meant everything to Viktor.

Where the hell is that bear shifter when I need him?

"My poor little, traumatized bride. Things certainly went awfully sideways last week when I sent my men to collect you, didn't they, my pet?" Conrad said loud enough so all the spectators could overhear, as he inched even closer to Halle, who seemed to have frozen in his clutches. "You poor thing, being forced into a mating by this criminal. Have no fear, I will free you from his bond and we will finally start our life together …just as your *family* intended."

Those ridiculous words seemed to knock Halle out of her stationary horror. Viktor hoped that she'd seen her brother safe behind him, and he could tell by the smug look on Conrad's face that his nemesis still hadn't spotted his newly liberated leverage. He prayed to the Goddess that Halle would trust that he would do anything in the future to protect the rest of her family from suffering the same fate as Tavin almost did. Viktor saw the flash of amber in her eyes as her cat rose to the surface.

"You're completely insane, Conrad. I choose Viktor. *He* is my mate." She spat back at him with a growl. "He saved me from *you*, and he saved my brother, too. I will never be your anything."

Viktor should have known that his little mate

would choose exactly the words that would hit the man where it would do the most damage, his ego. He was half proud and half furious as Conrad reacted exactly as Viktor knew he would to being verbally humiliated in public—he lost his shit.

Before Viktor or Halle could even react, Conrad swung her around, his claws now gripping around her throat tight enough that Viktor could smell the sweet scent of her precious blood. Viktor watched Conrad's eyes search frantically through the crowd, and he saw the surprise and then the rage when Tavin must have been spotted safe amongst the gawkers instead of tied up and guarded where Conrad had left him.

"Listen, bitch," Conrad whispered low in her ear. "You'll spend the rest of your life on your back ensuring my legacy, and when I have the heirs I need, then as far as I'm concerned, you'll be demoted to chew toy for the rest of my men."

They had drawn quite a crowd in the lobby at this point, and when the elevator dinged open and three large men stepped out, Viktor couldn't even guess what was about to happen. He did know, however, that if Conrad hurt his mate, he would kill him right in front of the Goddess herself and be damned if he cared about the consequences of who was watching.

The largest of the men stepped forward and approached Conrad with his hands raised like he was addressing a crazy person with a bomb.

"Conrad, what seems to be the trouble here? Why don't you let Miss Briggs go, and we can discuss this rationally?"

"Ah, Burton, thank goodness you're here." Conrad's tone changed instantly from the smarmy asshole to one of near comedic relief at the sight of the council member. "This rogue was trying to steal my fiancée once again. Have your enforcers arrest this animal!"

****

"Is this true, Miss Briggs?" The huge bear of a man looked pointedly at Halle.

"No," Halle tried to choke out before Conrad's fingers tightened once again on her throat. "Viktor is my mate. Conrad—"

Conrad cut off her air before she could finish. She heard Viktor's scramble to try to get to her, but he was now being held back by the two enforcers that had arrived in the elevator with Burton. Out of the corner of her eye, she saw a quick flash of black and grey and she remembered the words of advice that Dori had given her in the bathroom this morning. Obviously, these men weren't going to let Viktor save her, so she was just going to have to save herself. Part of this realization terrified her. It was true Halle's beast was a predator, but she'd never really been in a physical altercation before. Could she attack an ancient vampire who had the strength to rip her head from her body in the blink of an eye? All she could do was hope that his motivation for keeping her alive would hold fast. Halle had made her decision. She wasn't the biddable, simpering little woman that Conrad thought she was. She was a fucking leopard, and she wanted her mate.

The bastard's arm moved over the chain Molly had given her after breakfast and it caused a small wave of raw magic to be released, making tiny goosebumps emerge all over her body. Whatever it had done seemed to surprise Conrad as well, because he gasped and his arm slipped almost right up against her chin. So all she had to do was open up her mouth and take a big bite. She dug her claws in deep anywhere she could find purchase, the same instant that her fangs sank straight into the vampire's flesh until blood was gushing freely into her mouth.

Conrad roared and flung her out of his grasp, right into the path of the council member standing in front of them. The two vampires behind their coven leader looked as though they were ready to start killing at the damage done to their boss.

"You bitch!" he screamed, holding his arm that now had a ragged flap of bloody flesh hanging loose, courtesy of her leopard's sharp teeth. "You will pay for this. You *and* your entire family will pay. You still belong to me in payment for your father's blood debt!"

The large man who had caught Halle gently pushed her behind him and off towards Viktor's waiting arms.

"Actually, Conrad, you just attacked another male's registered mate. As you know, a true mating cannot be overturned by family contracts, even blood debts," Burton said to him, still watching him closely.

"They did not go upstairs for their appointment time with the council, so there was no registration!" Conrad spat back desperately, his well-groomed and controlled façade completely gone now.

"Hmm, and how exactly did you know they had an appointment, Conrad? Sounds like we have a leak somewhere, and that must have been how you managed to call this morning to make an appointment for yourself as well, correct? Regardless, I guess you could say that we're working on a new pre-registration program for fated mates," the bear answered back smugly as if he'd just been waiting to put Conrad in his place.

"Yes, and we called ahead," Viktor added, as he held Halle tight against him.

Halle was so happy to be safe back in Viktor's arms, she forgot all about the taste of that bastard's blood still lingering in her mouth. It was quite satisfying to see Conrad lose his grip on his well-practiced temper when Burton spoke, but when Viktor added his smug two cents, the coven leader full on snapped and lunged forward. Burton was a huge man. He had to be well over two hundred and fifty pounds, but Conrad batted him aside like he was nothing. The coven leader's goons went after one of the enforcers, and when the other tried to stop the angry vampire, Conrad went right for his throat, ripping it out like a wild animal.

Halle was shocked and horrified as she watched the young shifter's life slip out of his eyes as his blood spread out on the floor around him. It was terrifying to think that it had been her throat in Conrad's grip, not moments before. That it so easily could have been her lying there dying on the cold marble. This wasn't the way things were supposed to happen today. They were supposed to have their mating registered, and then go back home to Viktor's house to celebrate it in bed.

Could this really be happening?

Chapter Twenty-Four

Viktor watched as the true nature of his nemesis was revealed in his fury. The madness in Conrad's eyes as he attacked the young enforcer brought back memories from before his turning of what Melisandre's coven was capable of, memories that Viktor had hoped to forget forever.

Part of him wanted to flee with Halle, to take her somewhere safe away from his enemies, but the other part knew that meant leaving Burton, his enforcers, and Goddess knew how many other innocent lives to Conrad's madness—and he couldn't do it. He was shocked to realize that his relentless pursuit of vengeance against Conrad that had been plaguing him for his entire undead lifetime wasn't even a consideration in his decision-making. He did come to the conclusion, however, that the only way he could guarantee Halle's safety from Conrad once and for all would be to ensure that he was nothing more than ashes in the wind.

Viktor watched as Burton got back up and charged towards the vampire, only to be sent flying through the air and into the wall next to them. Viktor pushed Halle back to where the large man was now crumpled on the floor and he turned to Conrad, baring his fangs.

There was nothing pretty or clean about vampires fighting in hand-to-hand combat. Claws and teeth were sharp and swift, and when he collided with his enemy they were both moving at top speed, slashing at everything they could reach. Conrad was at least a century older than Viktor, and that meant he was faster and supernaturally stronger than Viktor, but he wasn't a soldier. He wasn't battle trained and warrior-bred—not like Viktor was.

Viktor much preferred to fight with his blades, but he was taking his time, methodically attacking Conrad's weakest points, enjoying each hiss of pain the other man relinquished while trying to ignore the sting of his own wounds.

He grunted as his opponent got in a lucky strike and Viktor felt the deep furrows from Conrad's claws open across his chest and dropped to one knee. Conrad must have been at the end of his energy because he tried to take advantage of Viktor's distraction by turning back to lunge in Halle's direction. He was no doubt hoping to use her as leverage to get out of this situation with his life, even if his role as Coven Master would be over.

Viktor saw Burton yell and toss a blade towards him. Viktor didn't even think, in a burst of adrenaline he leaped into the air, grabbing the knife before landing in front of his mate and slashing the metal with all his vampire strength at his target.

****

Halle gasped when she saw her mate fall to one knee, bright red marks seeping through his shirt, across his chest.

"Viktor!" she screamed as fear tightened her throat, and then suddenly the blur that was Conrad stopped and turned, stalking straight for her.

She heard Burton yell out beside her to Viktor. Halle saw him throw something in the air as her mate leaped in their direction, and then suddenly she couldn't see anything at all, except a wide back because she found herself shoved between Viktor and the elevator door.

She did, however, hear the grossest sound of thick blood spatter hitting the walls around her, and, for a second, she was frozen in fear that the blood belonged to the man she loved. Panic gripped her, and she struggled to keep control of her body as her leopard fought to take over and protect them both.

Then, as suddenly as the violence had erupted, it was over, and the lobby was as quiet as a tomb in the aftermath.

"Holy hell, Krescech." Burton whistled as he slowly got to his feet and walked over to where Viktor and Halle were now standing in front of Conrad's headless body. "You had me worried there for a little bit. I wasn't sure we were going to be able to pull this off. But once you had that blade you just lopped off his head like he was standing still."

"Yes, well, Conrad may have been older than me, but he was never much of a fighter," Viktor answered, as he checked Halle over to see if she was all right. "He had always been too arrogant to train and work for anything. His specialty was always running away and hiding behind others."

Suddenly, the entire lobby swarmed with enforcers.

"Where the hell have you been, Garreth?" Burton snarled at the large wolf shifter as they knelt down to their fallen men. "Get a healer here now. Kent's still alive."

"Yes, sir. Belinda's right behind me. We were delayed by Conrad's men. They set up a distraction at the East entrance to the building," the other man said, as a small female pushed him out of the way and began to heal the man on the ground.

"Take care of this mess. I'll get them upstairs," was all Burton said before he looked back at them.

"That's just creepy as hell," Burton muttered, bringing Viktor's attention back to the body at their feet that was just slowly beginning to turn to ash starting from the edges of the wounds inwards. "Why is it going so slowly compared to the other two?"

"Vampires that are as old as Conrad are full of power and magic, and as the Goddess takes back what was given after death, the aging process catches up with the cells. The older the vampire, the more magic must be reabsorbed, so the longer it takes the body to break down."

"I've never seen that before." The other man seemed transfixed as he watched Conrad's body turn to ash, layer by layer.

"Most of the ancients know better than to get themselves killed in front of a crowd," Viktor sighed. "The others will not be impressed that I did this here with so many witnesses."

"Better him than us, my friend." Burton finally seemed to be able to take his eyes away from Conrad's fading body.

Chapter Twenty-Five

"Halle!"

Viktor tensed and shoved Halle behind him until he seemed to recognize that it was her brother yelling out for her as he tried to push his way through the crowd of onlookers.

"Tavin?" Burton cringed when he saw the tattered and bloodstained clothes her brother was in as he gathered his sister into a tight hug, "Good Goddess, you look like shit. What in the hell happened to you?"

"That's how Dair got his hands back on Halle this morning as we were coming to our appointment. He was threatening to kill Tavin unless she came and signed the papers with him," Viktor explained.

"I had wondered about that when I saw them listed in the appointment book. I have to find out who that bastard bribed to get in here this morning." Burton frowned and looked towards the body of his fallen comrade laying on the stone floor. "Someone will pay for this, Jackson was a good man."

"I'm so glad you're okay, Tavin." Halle ran her hands over her brother's arms, checking to see that his wounds were beginning to heal. "You need to go home and rest."

"Burton, do you have someone that can take Tavin home?" her mate asked, and she rewarded him for his thoughtfulness with a smile.

The Council member called over a couple of enforcers to help and escort Tavin home, and as soon as she watched her brother safely leave the building Halle was burrowed back into his arms once again. She noticed that Viktor turned her away from what was left of Conrad's body, which was just fine. She didn't want to have to look at that bastard ever again.

"Well, shall we go upstairs and complete your registration?" Burton asked, rubbing his hands together like they weren't talking over the decapitated corpse of an evil sociopath that was slowly turning to ash. "I think I've got a business proposition for you, Viktor."

"Do you have somewhere we can clean up first?" Viktor asked, frowning at her. He appeared to be fixated on the amount of blood spatter that had hit Halle, not to mention the healing wounds that were still showing on her throat from Conrad's claws. Her hand moved back up to her throat as she remembered his nails digging into her skin. When she brushed against the amulet that Molly had given her at breakfast, another small wave of magic flowed from it—but this time it was a soothing balm on her tattered nerves. She certainly couldn't claim to understand the wild nature of the Brownie's magic, but she was thankful for it all the same.

The elevator doors dinged open, and Dori was already standing inside, causing the two men to curse and Halle to jump in surprise. *Damned tricky fairies.*

"Goddess, Pandora, I told you that you can't just pop into the Council building. You shouldn't even have the ability to *do* that with the wards we've paid for around here!" Burton yelled at the little goth fairy in a tone that clearly implied that he'd known her for some time, as the three of them joined her in the elevator to go upstairs.

"Sure thing, Huggie Bear. I'm just here to take care of my charges and I'll be right out of your hair," she answered with a wink before she waved her little wand that looked suspiciously like a riding crop.

Halle had to stifle a grin at the look that crossed Burton's face when he noticed what Dori was waving at him. It was a bizarre mixture of sexual interest, embarrassment, and then confusion. She knew that Dori didn't need a wand to use her magic, as she hadn't had one at any other time that Halle had seen her use her abilities, so she assumed that the prop was for the handsome bear shifter's benefit … or simply for her own amusement.

Seconds later, she felt Dori's magic roll through the entire space of the elevator, and suddenly she found herself in a brand-new dress. Once again sans undergarments—*cheeky fairy.* When she looked over at Viktor, she had to do a double take, as he was now dressed in tight black leather pants and a body molding black t-shirt. Since she'd only seen him wear dress shirts and slacks, this bad-boy version of her mate really kicked up her libido. The look on his face once he realized what Dori had done was the best part, though. He looked down and cringed as he flexed a little in his new pants.

"Was this really necessary, Fairy?" Viktor growled out, as he tried to casually find a comfortable way to stand in the skin-tight leather pants.

"As the female contingent in this elevator can attest to, *hell yeah* it was necessary. I've been fantasizing about you in skin-tight leather ever since I first saw you in the bar," Dori said with a wink.

"Hey!"

Halle turned her eyes away from her delectable mate just long enough to protest the statement and hear Burton's laugh at the red flush that flared across Viktor's cheeks.

"Relax, sweets," the fairy answered her with hands up. "I had him tagged for you right from the start. I never would've touched!"

****

"Why are you here, Fairy?" Viktor asked, as the elevator doors swung open, and they all walked out into the council chamber foyer, his head still spinning from how quickly everything had just happened. It was almost too good to believe that Conrad was finally dead and Halle was safe and relatively unharmed.

"You've just been Fairy Godmothered, hotness. No need to thank me." Pandora stood looking very impressed with herself. "Welcome to your Happy Ever After, Viktor."

With those final words, the odd little woman magically popped back out of the room, leaving Burton once again cursing and yelling down the hall to his tech witches about the damn wards and how useless they were if a tiny fairy could get in and out at will.

Halle's delicate snort of laughter brought his attention back to her, and he pulled her into his arms. When he ran his hands down her back, he couldn't stifle the growl when he noticed that she wasn't wearing any bra or panties.

"We need to leave," he whispered in her ear, as he lightly nibbled on her delicate neck.

"What? We just got up here, Viktor," she giggled as he must have hit a ticklish spot. "And after all that, we still have to see the council and complete our registration. Then we can go home and lock ourselves in your bedroom for a couple of days."

"Burton! Hurry up!" Viktor yelled down the hall as he yanked Halle into the council chambers.

The big bear came running back down the hall and around the corner.

"Bad news, guys, the council was evacuated when the alarm was triggered at Conrad's attack. But the good news is that I can file your paperwork on my own once you sign it, now that he's out of the picture and there's no one to contest your mating."

"Then why are we still here?" Viktor growled as he signed the forms Burton gave them, then handed the pen to Halle to do the same, while the shifter stood grinning in front of them.

"You guys can go on home now," Burton answered, still smiling at him for some unknown reason. "But I still have that proposition for you that we need to discuss, so I'll call you next week, okay?"

"Fine, let's go home, Halle," Viktor said, as he swept Halle off her feet and carried her back out to the elevator.

When the elevator doors closed leaving the too cheery bear on the other side, Viktor pulled Halle in close for a slow kiss. He had no idea why he'd been given such a gift as to have her as his mate, but never would he take it for granted. As they continued to kiss, his hands wandered down to her ass and once again he was reminded that she wasn't wearing any panties. He moaned and pushed her back against the wall, letting her feel what she did to his body.

"It's nice to see that my undergarments weren't the only ones that ridiculous Fairy forgot when she conjured our new clothing," he whispered, nibbling on her neck again as she rubbed herself against his hard shaft.

"Ugh, that's the second time she's done that to me! Dori seems to think it's hilarious. But to tell you the truth, I don't mind so much at the moment," she said with a mischievous smile, as she slid her fingers down the front of his pants, teasing him.

"I guess I can't fault the fairy for her results, can I?" he whispered an inch away from her lips.

"Nope, now let's see if you can give me a 'happy ending' before we reach the lobby," Halle whispered back before she grabbed Viktor's hand and slid it up her thigh, under the hem of her dress to where she was aching for him.

"Anything for you, mate," was his answer before he brought his lips back to hers.

Chapter Twenty-Six

Dori may have still been eavesdropping on the delectable male she loved to vex when she had the time to drop by, so when she heard him muttering her name to himself in the now empty foyer, she popped back in front of him.

"Dori! How are you even able to get through the wards in here?" Burton yelled before he spotted the blonde witch trying to sneak down the hall unseen. "You! How come this fairy can get through the wards we pay you to maintain?"

"Um, she can't," the witch stuttered. "She must be getting inside help from another witch, or an empowered object of some type. Hey—why don't I stay late and we can try to figure this out together?"

Dori didn't like the way the witch sidled up to Burton, batting her lashes and pushing her cleavage together.

"You skank!"

How dare this ho make a play for the bear I've tentatively set aside for when I am maybe ready to settle down...

"This power," Dori ran her hands down her black corset top and was well rewarded as Burton's eyes moved along with them, "is one hundred percent natural, biotch, unlike *some* things..."

Dori nodded towards the ridiculous double d's threatening to capsize the petite blonde. The witch's eyes darted towards the man in between them, her mouth dropping open in shock.

"What? I'd know a pair of magically enhanced tatas from a mile away," Dori sneered as her eyes narrowed in threat towards the other woman, "Now beat it. He's not interested in what you've got on 'mark down',

Wicca Barbie."

She kept her eyes on the witch as she retreated down the hallway from which she came—one never could be too careful with those shifty witches, especially when you just insulted said witch. That sort of thing usually got you a hex thrown your way as soon as you turned your back.

"What was that?" Burton's tone was no longer angry. In fact, it seemed curious, and if she had to guess, rather amused.

"What?" She tried to brush off her little territorial slap-fight. "Human Resources around here should really rethink their sexual harassment orientations. That was *very* inappropriate."

His annoyingly perfect eyebrows lifted even further up his forehead. "Were you jealous?"

"Jealous? Hah, who knows which of her cheesy lines you would have fallen for if I hadn't been here." She pretended to study her nails. "Those witches are sexual predators."

"Hmm, want to keep me all to yourself, do you?" The small smile that crept onto his lips was utterly adorable and temporarily distracted her from what he had said—but then it hit her.

Eeeks! The bear knows too much! Retreat! Retreat!

Dori took a big step back and told herself that clearly, with such a wildly successful launch of her new business, she didn't have the time or energy to play with handsome bear shifters—especially busybody, know-it-all bear shifters that held a seat on the Para Council.

"Oh wow, would you look at that time?" She glanced down at the studded leather wraparound bracelet that adorned her left wrist. "Super busy with my new career, gotta jet. I'll send you some business cards for referrals. Thanks, Burton!"

She looked up a fraction of a second before she used her magic to take her back home, and Dori hated the fact that the knowing smile on that bear's face made her heartbeat stutter in her chest.

That one's going to be trouble, I just know it.

Chapter Twenty-Seven

A few months later

"You look like you could use a little break from the festivities, babe." Halle stifled a grin at the look of dejection on her mate's face right now. When her mother had said they'd be having a small gathering to officially celebrate their mating, she hadn't had the heart to warn him that her mom's idea of a "small gathering" was going to seem like the sixth level of hell to someone who'd spent years isolating himself. "Come with me, I have something I want to show you."

"Gladly." He took her offered hand and followed her up the stairs and down the long hallway, away from the crowd until they came to a familiar door with her name in letters on the front. Halle's pulse skipped a beat at the look of heat she saw in her mate's eyes as he slowly shut the bedroom door closed behind them.

"Well, you wanted to see my old bedroom, and here it is." Her voice was a sultry purr, imagining all the dirty things she wanted to do to him in here. It was exciting to think that there was a house full of people downstairs completely oblivious to what they might get up to.

"Hmm, what a naughty little thing you are, tempting me to ravage you in your childhood bedroom while anyone could walk in and catch us." This particular smile he gave her was a favorite—it usually happened before he did something deliciously kinky, and kitty liked her some kink. Her new mate had decided to take her sensual education firmly in hand and teach her *everything* she'd been missing out on … and there had been *so* much she'd been missing out on.

"Oh, I am super naughty—I think that maybe you should punish me." She blinked up innocently at him.

"Punish you?" His low laugh made goosebumps break out all over her skin in anticipation. "Come now, sweet, if I were to do that the entire house would know what we were up to because you'd be screaming my name."

Halle's breathing became heavy as Viktor stalked closer, backing her up against the wall slowly until his body was so close to hers she could feel the heat coming off of him.

"No, I think I will wait to punish you until we get home." He ran a fingertip gently from her cheek, trailing it down her neck, following the deep V neckline of her wrap dress. His fingers tugged slowly on the tie until it released and the soft green material fell to the sides of her body, revealing the lace bra and panties, "For now, I want you on your knees."

A warm pulse of excitement rushed through her body at his words. Halle loved it when Viktor took charge in the bedroom. She was only just discovering the freedom of submitting to him, and it was thrilling. Her body quickened, moisture pooling between her thighs as she dropped to her knees before him on the thick carpeting.

"Take out my cock," he commanded, his voice thick with desire.

Halle slowly ran her fingers along the thick ridge of his desire beneath the expensive material of his dress pants, and she could feel his flesh jerk under her fingertips before she undid the closure and lowered the zipper. The low groan from her mate as she licked her lips was music to her ears, and when his thick shaft sprang forth she wasted no time in leaning forward to collect the drop of moisture beading at the tip with her tongue.

"Mmm, that's right, baby, suck me down." He

moaned as she took his length into her mouth, swirling her tongue along as she went, savoring the taste of him. Halle suckled and moved along his shaft with enthusiasm, the tension in his thighs under her hands letting her know exactly how much he was enjoying her mouth on him. "Ahh, fuck, babe. That's so good, but I need to be inside you before I can go back out there and deal with that."

She wanted him, too, so she relinquished his cock with a loud pop, and then he was lifting her up to lay on the edge of the bed. Halle lifted her arms up above her head, and he smiled in approval, as he slowly pulled her panties down her legs and dropped them to the floor.

"Keep those arms up, and show me what's mine," he growled as he pushed her bra up and over her breasts, palming the sensitive flesh in his strong hands.

Halle spread her legs wide open, revealing her swollen folds to the man that she loved. Viktor fell to his knees beside the bed, his hands grabbing her knees and jerking her closer towards him. She had to bite her lip to stop the moan that threatened to break forth as he leaned forward and took a long lick from her drenched opening all the way up to her sensitive clit. A small whimper escaped her when one of his fangs circled the swollen nub, and he chuckled.

"Quiet, remember, baby? You don't want your mom catching us in here, do you?"

"Ugh, please don't talk about my mom when your mouth is on my pussy, okay?" Her voice was trembling, due to the fact that he was still teasing her clit.

"Fair enough," he answered before he kissed his way back up her stomach and along her breasts until he finally reached her mouth. His kiss was slow and sensual as his tongue teased hers. Halle moaned as she felt the fat head of his cock slide through her folds until he found her entrance and slowly pressed inside. She felt every inch of him, and though her hands itched to trace over his beautiful body, she kept them above her head as she'd been instructed to. His thrusts were drawn out and deliberate, and she sucked on his tongue as it invaded her mouth and was rewarded as his hips began a faster pace.

"Is this what you want, little one?" He pulled his mouth away to watch her face intently as he fucked her harder.

"Yes, I need to come," she whimpered, her fingers thrashing in the battle to follow his instruction. "Please, Viktor!"

He said nothing in return. He simply brought one finger down to circle her aching clit as he thrust into her faster and faster, all the while, watching her face like he'd never seen anything so enthralling.

"I love watching you as you come apart for me, baby." He finally placed his thumb over her clit and rubbed furiously as his hips slammed against hers.

Halle was thankful that he dove down to cover her mouth with his in a soul-stealing kiss as the pleasure crested inside of her and she shattered around the length of him. Otherwise, the entire house would have heard her scream his name as she came. He thrust a few more times inside of her before he pushed deep and a ragged moan joined hers as he followed her into bliss.

****

"I can't believe you talked me into accepting this job, love." Viktor sighed as he pulled at his tie once again.

Halle knew he would've stayed the entire evening held up in her room if it had been up to him, but she'd simply laughed thinking that it had been a minor miracle already that her mom hadn't sent someone to track them down. They'd reluctantly gotten dressed and headed back down to the party.

He obligingly nodded to various people he didn't know as the strangers said hello, and he held Halle's arm as they walked through the lavish ballroom.

"It's a great opportunity, both for you and the rest of the covens here. I think you're going to do a fantastic job as the new Coven Leader of North America. Conrad was such a douchebag that most of the older vamps had just left altogether. We've already gotten hundreds of petitions for members to return back to your territory," Halle said, as she sipped from her glass of champagne. "You don't give yourself enough credit, Viktor. You're a very competent and fair leader. Otherwise, Burton would never have recommended you for the position in the first place."

"I'm so lucky you're willing to help me with all of this. You've got a gift for dealing with others, Halle," he answered while still trying to smile at strangers. "I'm still not quite used to so much socializing after keeping to myself for so many years, and there's just so many … people."

Halle laughed at the tone of his voice. He sounded like he'd just found something disgusting stuck to the bottom of his very expensive shoes. She had to agree, though, at least on the number of sheer people that had attended tonight. Her parents had gone overboard on their party, and she knew there would only be more to come. Viktor had wanted to get married, and Halle was fine either way. Most shifters usually had a party once they mated, so her mother had been ecstatic at her first opportunity to plan an actual full on wedding with all the bells and whistles. Plus, with Viktor's new appointment to Coven Leader, it meant, even more people they didn't know wanted to congratulate them and come to celebrate. All the socializing was practically giving her mate hives.

"Well, I warned you, baby, shifter parents aren't really good with boundaries. I told you we should've bought a house in a city that was farther away from the pard," she answered right before her mother snuck up behind them and grabbed the glass right out of her hand.

"Hey! I was drinking that!" Halle protested, as her mother just ignored her and beamed up at Viktor.

"This has been such a lovely turn out, Viktor. Everyone seems to be pleased as punch that you accepted the Coven Leader position," she cooed before she downed the rest of Halle's champagne. "And all the other ladies in my wine club are beside themselves with jealousy that my Halle has mated herself such a handsome and important male!"

The exaggerated eye roll Halle gave her mom was totally ignored by the older woman, of course.

"Really, Mom, how do you manage to make *everything* about you?" Halle asked as she flagged down another server with a tray of drinks.

Her mother grabbed a smaller glass off the tray filled with pink sparkling juice and handed it to her with a pointed look.

"You shouldn't be drinking in your condition, sweetheart. I don't want to take any chances with my grandcub," her mother gushed, right before catching sight of someone she knew and rushed off to gossip.

Halle heard the crack of the crystal glass in Viktor's hand, and she felt like an idiot for not realizing sooner why she'd been so queasy for the last couple of weeks. They'd barely been mated for three months and so much had changed for Viktor in his life, she was almost scared to look up and see his reaction to the news that she was pregnant.

"Truly, Halle?" he whispered in a quiet voice.

She finally looked up to see the tears in his eyes,

and with the sheer look of wonder on his face, all her fears evaporated.

"Well, I haven't taken a test or been to the doctor, but my mom's nose never lies. Are you happy about this, Viktor?" she asked, as she took his hand in hers.

"I am ... surprised." He seemed to be struggling to find his words. "Of course I realized that it was possible..."

Halle began to worry that this was too much, too fast for her mate. Vampires as a rule did not usually procreate as the amount of extra blood a female would have to consume to carry a child to term was tedious—she'd done a little research on that when her father had told her about Conrad. But it *had* happened. She and Viktor hadn't talked about children once they'd mated. They were too busy enjoying themselves—hence the bun currently in her oven. Halle wanted to be excited about the life they'd created, but would Viktor be? He must have seen the concern in her face as he smiled and quickly took her hands in his own.

"I never imagined in my wildest fantasies that I could be as happy as you make me, Halle," he answered, pulling her in close to press a soft kiss to her lips. "I never dreamed that I would once again be blessed with a family of my own."

"I guess we should both send Dori a fruit basket or something then, huh?"

"I think she stole my car from where we left it en route to the Council Building that morning. When we arrived back home that afternoon, I found a note in the pocket of those ridiculously tight leather pants that said, *'You missed the last oil change on your Aston Martin, and your door fell off. You really should take better care of such a beautiful machine. But no worries, sweet cheeks, I have the perfect mechanic to take care of it!'*

She has yet to return it, so I guess we'll just call it even then," he said, as he hugged his mate close and secretly thanked his Fairy Godmother.

And they lived Happily Ever After.

Epilogue

"I have to admit, girl, I never thought you'd pull this off."

Dori's Nana just stood there in the kitchen while she had the oddest expression on her face. It was almost, a smile?

"Gee, thanks, Nan." Dori just rolled her eyes and went back to the debacle she was working on at the kitchen table.

She was surprised when the chair next to her pulled out and her grandmother sat down.

"So what's your plan now? Are you picking the next name or are you going to advertise on the para black market?"

Good grief, Dori had never heard her grandmother sound so excited about anything, ever. Could it be the old battle-ax had finally gotten bored of society gossip and endless rounds of cribbage? Pandora just looked over at the woman for a moment with a measuring stare.

"You want *in*, Nana?"

"Well, you're clearly going to need some help if you expect not to get caught by the Fairy God Council. I *did* date every single one of them. So, I can make sure they're looking the other way," Nana said as she tried to look coy and primped her hair.

"*All* of them Nana? Even that ass-hat Basil?" Dori tried to hide the fact that she was secretly impressed with her grandmother's promiscuous ways, cringing when she accidentally imagined the super old Grand-Fairy Council Master Basil buck-ass naked.

Ugh. There were some things you just never wanted to imagine.

"We all make mistakes, dear," she answered with

a wink, right before Dori's mom burst into the kitchen.

"Why in the heck is my office all pulled apart, young lady?" Dori's mom yelled as she walked into the kitchen and stood there with her hands on her hips looking serious at least for a moment until she saw what her daughter was doing. "Are you writing a *letter* on stationery?"

"Yes, and let me tell you, my handwriting is *not* what it used to be," Dori sighed as she crumpled up the sheet she'd been working on and started another.

Cripes, no wonder the computer had been invented! It would have taken people ages to get anything done if they had to write stuff down on paper all the time. Not to mention the gross ink smudges all along her skin due to her superior left-handed awesomeness.

"Well, I'm certainly not one to condone a waste of magic, as you know," her mother said, as she plunked down in the chair across from her, "but why on Earth don't you just create one if you have to, instead of writing it by hand?"

"Trust me, I would if that was an option, but he *always* smells the magic and refuses to open any correspondence that hasn't been done completely manually."

"*He* who, my dear?" her Nana asked while getting up to pour herself a cup of coffee. "I can't imagine why you'd go to this much trouble for anyone."

"*He* is Barrett, my mechanic. I need to bring Viktor's car in for a repair," Dori said, as she very carefully signed her name to the completed request for an appointment time when she could call him. "He's an ogre with some severe OCD issues, and trust me, you do *not* want to surprise him in any way. He has a tendency to get a little *Hulk-Smash-y* when he's startled."

Dori folded the letter in half and handed it to her

mother carefully like she was afraid she'd accidentally trip and spill coffee on it or something.

"Can you please take this to the post office and mail it to the address at the top?"

"Sure." Her mom agreed and then flipped open the letter to read what her daughter had written.

"What? You're asking him for an appointment time so that you can then *text* him to make another appointment time to be able to *call* him?" Tabitha asked in disbelief, looking back at her daughter. "Is this guy crazy, or what?"

"Look, Mom, I told you he's got some issues. But he's literally the best mechanic on the West Coast ... and as long as he doesn't see me coming, he's also going to be our next client."

The End

www.sarahmarshfiction.com

SARAH MARSH

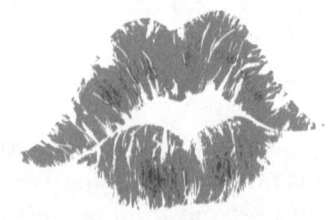

EVERNIGHT PUBLISHING ®

www.evernightpublishing.com

www.ingramcontent.com/pod-product-compliance
Lightning Source LLC
Chambersburg PA
CBHW022028170626
46808CB00003B/1100